BORDER CROSSING

**ALSO BY
JESSICA LEE ANDERSON**

Trudy

BORDER CROSSING

Jessica Lee Anderson

milkweed
editions

The characters and events in this book are fictitious. Any similarity to real persons, living or dead, is coincidental and not intended by the author.

Published 2009 by Milkweed Editions
Printed in Canada
Cover design by Lee Design
Cover photo by Maria Teijeiro/Getty
Author photo by Tim Kingsbury
Interior design by Steve Foley
The text of this book is set in Emona.
09 10 11 12 13 5 4 3 2 1
First Edition

Please turn to the back of this book for a list of the sustaining funders of Milkweed Editions.

Library of Congress Cataloging-in-Publication Data

Anderson, Jessica Lee, 1980-
 Border crossing / Jessica Lee Anderson. — 1st ed.
     p. cm.
 Summary: Manz, a troubled fifteen-year-old, ruminates over his Mexican father's death, his mother's drinking, and his stillborn stepbrother until the voices he hears in his head take over and he cannot tell reality from delusion.
 ISBN 978-1-57131-689-9 (hardcover : alk. paper) — ISBN 978-1-57131-691-2 (pbk. : alk. paper)
 [1. Schizophrenia—Fiction. 2. Mental illness—Fiction. 3. Alcoholism—Fiction. 4. Racially mixed people—Fiction.] I. Title.
 PZ7.A53665Bo 2009
 [Fic]—dc22
                          2008049408

This book is printed on acid-free paper.

For Michael

BORDER CROSSING

ACKNOWLEDGMENTS

SO MANY FOLKS CONTRIBUTED their time, talent, and energy to this book. I feel particularly fortunate to have Ben Barnhart as my editor once again. He is patient, extremely insightful, and a joy to work with. Thanks to all the wonderful folks at Milkweed for their hard work and vision. I am also grateful to have John Silbersack as my agent.

I'm indebted to my parents for their love and support. Had they not driven me hundreds of miles to attend Sul Ross State University, I doubt this book would be a reality. Thanks to Brian Colunga and Pete Martinez for their stories and friendship. Thanks to Dr. Mark Saka as well for sharing his knowledge and teaching history so honestly.

I'm also indebted to Han Nolan, an incredible writer and mentor. Manz's story took shape under her guidance. I must acknowledge Hollins University's excellent children's literature program and would like to additionally thank Dr. Lisa Rowe Fraustino and Amanda Cockrell. I could never forget Ann Sullivan and will hold her storytelling lessons dear to my heart.

I will be forever grateful to Schizophrenia.com for the wealth of information available and the sense of community offered.

And lastly, thanks to my best friend and husband, Michael Anderson. He carefully read the manuscript and believed in the story even when I had my doubts.

BORDER CROSSING

ONE OF THOSE NIGHTS

My room blazed red. Before I heard the car door slam I sniffed the air for traces of smoke, but the red glow was nothing more than the reflection of brake lights through the window. It wasn't the thought of flames that scared me. It was the thought that I might stay in bed and do nothing about it.

My head pounded as if it were separate from my heart, and my temples throbbed as I watched the car back out of the driveway. The clock glowed 2:17 A.M. Just like my mother. Delores. The grinding of keys in the lock and her banging on the door made me hope the driver wasn't as drunk as she was.

Delores pushed her way into the house after the lock snapped open. "Manz?" she called out.

I didn't say anything. I listened as her purse crashed to the floor. Something rolled out.

"Manz?"

Her heels clomped on the ceramic tile, and when I heard them pause, I knew she was standing outside of Gabriel's room.

"I'm awake," I said. My heart was still racing.

I could smell the gas station fried chicken and ashtrays as she entered my room. "Did you make anything to eat?" she asked.

If Tom had been there he would've gotten out of bed to microwave her something. But Tom wasn't there.

"There's some rice in the fridge."

She didn't head for the kitchen, though. I felt a slight shift in the mattress as she sat on the edge of my bed. Whiskey fumed from her pores and her mouth. I took shallow breaths to minimize the stench.

"Got stuck working late."

Working doesn't smell like this, I thought. The light from the hallway spilled into the room and illuminated her blonde-streaked hair. Her reddish lipstick was smeared underneath her lip, making her look like a clown.

"Tom called when you were out," I said, lying. I wasn't sure why I even said it. Tom wrote a letter for every day that he'd be gone on the road. He rarely called, but Delores was too drunk tonight to realize it. He took us in years ago. At first it was a crush and a place to crash, but then it became permanent.

"Tonight? Whad'ya tell him?"

"That you were painting a picture. Of Gabriel." My lungs tightened as I said his name.

I watched as the color drained from her face. The red

of her lipstick grew more apparent. Delores stared at me and then looked toward Gabriel's room. The thick mascara around her eyes framed the hurt. "You been acting sick. Just like your father," she said, her words slurred. They stung.

Delores stood up and staggered out of my room. I heard her sobs, which started slowly at first, but the momentum built. She was in Gabriel's room.

I wasn't sure if Delores knew I'd seen the drawings of the baby before. His room transformed from a nursery to an art studio after he was gone. Paintings filled Gabriel's crib. Delores made it known she didn't want me in there. Not even Tom. Some days, I couldn't stay out. I couldn't keep from staring at the marble box holding his ashes.

I found the sketches of Gabriel while looking for some paint near the changing table. In the paintings, he looked like a perfect baby.

I BURIED MY FACE in the pillow, taking in my sour scent as my hot tears fell into the pillowcase. I tried to get myself to stop. Real guys don't cry. But I hadn't felt real for a long time.

I listened as she walked into the bathroom. She blew her nose and squeaked the bathroom faucet on and off. Then everything was quiet except for the humming of my nervousness. I imagined her body curled around the toilet and hoped she was breathing.

Vomit sprayed into the toilet and I sighed; she was breathing, for the moment at least. An hour passed, maybe two, and her snores filled the house. The humming stopped.

But I couldn't fall asleep. I stared at the shadows cascading on the wall. One shape stared back at me. A triangle that reminded me of something. A face?

I had to go to the bathroom, but I preferred the pain in my bladder to the thought of seeing Delores. I wondered how long things had been so bad between us.

When I was younger, I used to forget she was my mother. She was sixteen when I was born and I called her Delores. Maybe she pretended I was her brother instead of her son. Not like a name could lessen her obligation, but sometimes I wondered if she wished it could. I thought about what Gabriel would've called her. Probably not Delores.

Delores's father had disowned her—not when he found out she was pregnant, but when he found out she was pregnant by a Mexican. Her mother tried defending her, but like always, it was a battle lost. So for Delores, her life of running away started and ended in Rockhill, Texas. For me, it felt like things were ending a little more each day.

I was ready for my life of running to begin so I could finally get out of my head.

The face on the wall stared at me. I couldn't erase the image in my mind. I realized I couldn't remember my father's face anymore.

The toilet flushed, and the humming returned when I heard Delores crying. I couldn't talk to her about Gabriel. I walked out into the black of the night, the air stilted and stifling, and pissed by the side of the house.

ONE OF THOSE DAYS

"Can I get a ride?" Delores asked, cracking my bedroom door open. She smiled at me. Fake or not, when she smiled it reminded me that she was still young.

I thought about what would happen if I said no. If she didn't have to work, she might start painting again. She seemed more peaceful with a palette and paintbrush. I pulled at a hangnail.

"Please?" Delores smoothed out her wrinkled shirt and tied on her blue apron. The ties were so long they wrapped around her waist twice.

"Fine." I stayed in bed a moment longer and yawned. After fumbling through a stack of clothes in the corner of my room, I chose my favorite pair of jeans and a dark blue T-shirt. I slipped the jeans on, the cotton yellowed and thin around the knees.

As I pulled the shirt over my head my shoulder popped

so loud it seemed to echo. I took a corner of the inside of my shirt and polished my teeth clean.

Delores stuck her head into my room. "You ready, Isaiah?"

My ears burned at the sound of my birth name. For as long as I could remember, I was Manz. My father was Loco. Delores was always Delores. Thomas was Tom. Gabriel would've been Gabe.

I looked into the mirror before we left. The image staring back seemed nothing like me. My reflection looked as if I'd been crying. My heart beat off rhythm and I heard that humming noise again. I rubbed my hands over my eyes, but they were dry. I pulled the mirror off the wall and held it in my shaking hands and turned to see if Delores witnessed anything, but she was in the kitchen. I glanced in the mirror again, but this time, the reflection just showed my face—a face that looked like it was trying to make sense of things.

I let the mirror slip from my hands and watched as it fell to the ground. I didn't dare pick it up in case the glass wasn't shattered. How many years of bad luck does that bring, anyway?

"Manz, hurry up," Delores fussed.

I went into the bathroom and splashed water over my face. What was the matter with me?

My heart beat heavily as we got into the black Nova. I fought for my breath, the dry summer heat sucking it away. I turned the key, stepped on the gas, and felt the weight of the car as I threw it in reverse. I headed down Allen Street and passed by the railroad tracks—Rockhill's Great Divide.

Delores turned and faced me, but the wind through the open windows made it difficult to hear what she said. She looked so serious I thought she might've acknowledged something from last night.

"We should've left twenty minutes ago," she said, this time loud enough for me to hear. I should've known she wouldn't talk about last night on her own.

"It's only nine-fifteen. You won't be late." I wasn't sure why she cared so much about a job that paid a dollar over minimum wage. After the success of her last art show, she quit painting and got her old job back at the Mart. Tom encouraged her to keep up her art, but she said she felt drained and needed a break. "I like meeting people," she said, and apparently she met people at the Mart.

After giving birth to Gabriel, Delores spent three weeks in bed. Tom turned down two jobs to stay with her. I was grateful. I couldn't have handled it by myself.

If her mother hadn't died around that time, I don't think Delores would've ever crawled out of bed. When Tom told her the news, she said she wanted to go to the funeral, alone. So Tom bought Delores a plane ticket to Amarillo. He even packed her bags. Before she left, she kissed us each on the forehead and said nothing but, "I'm scared."

I wasn't sure what she was scared about. Maybe it was going home after all those years. Maybe it was the thought of seeing her father's grave at her mother's funeral. I didn't know and didn't ask; I hugged her instead and said, "Then don't leave."

When she returned home from the funeral Delores said she wanted to take an art class, so Tom helped her enroll and bought her over $300 worth of art supplies. After so much death, Delores seemed alive again. I never thought she had that kind of talent. I think it even caught her by surprise when she got an offer to display her work at the Blue Horn Gallery and got interviewed for a newspaper article.

The trip must've meant something to her. Her paintings were all from the viewpoint of a passenger looking out an airplane window. The painting that the newspaper praised the most made you feel as if you were looking over your shoulder. Out the window there was nothing but blackness. But if you looked closely enough, you could see a group of lights from a town, as if it were a cluster of stars instead. I felt cold looking at it.

The painting I liked showed a wing in the corner. A plane flew above the clouds. The painting's sky was tinted the color of the nursery walls and the clouds glowed from the setting sun. The painting made me think the distance from the plane to the ground wasn't so great.

I'd never flown in an airplane. I loved to drive and always traveled on the ground. Tom too. Tom hauled his semi across the United States, never really counting the miles. Delores sometimes teased him that his love for truck driving was greater than his love for her. The hairy man laughed and joked that it was true, but he always made his way back to Rockhill, back to Delores and me.

I don't think I could've faced coming back to this nothingness. I wanted out of there. As simple as that. Away from Rockhill and everyone there. Away from it all.

DELORES STARED OUT AT an orchard as I drove her to work. "Leaves look brown. The apples don't look as large as I remember from last year."

"None of it seems the same to me." And that was the truth; everything felt different, inside of me and out.

Rockhill used to be nothing but livestock before apple farming was introduced to the area almost half a century ago. Now there were over two hundred thousand apple trees. And plenty of migrant workers arriving every year. My father was one of them, bringing Delores and me with him as we traveled everywhere—packing light and staying tired, hungry, and thirsty. That was the same year of the fire blight when bacteria wiped out some of the orchards. Then it was the heat and drought.

I pulled into the chalky parking lot of Jackson's Food Mart, one of the two gas stations in Rockhill, known simply as the Mart. The competitor was on the other side of the tracks.

Right as I pulled into the lot, the white flash of a chicken ran past my headlights.

"Watch out!" Delores yelled.

I slammed on the brakes as a young boy chased after it, never thinking that a car might hit him.

As the boy was about to grab the chicken, it ran back

in front of the Nova. Delores and I sat in the idle car and watched the commotion. Jay Jackson walked out of the Mart and jammed his fists into the air. "Get away from here!"

Looking at the kid, I felt sorry for him. That could've been Gabriel chasing after something. Anything.

I ignored Jay Jackson and parked the black boat without pulling all the way into the spray painted parking slot.

Delores glanced over at Jay and got out of the car cautiously. I followed her.

"Don't you cause any trouble," she said, practically hissing. "You didn't forget about your little episode last year, did you?"

I didn't say anything, but Delores liked to remind me of the things I'd done. I should've been more aggressive about getting on her case. Maybe things would've been different.

I teamed up with the kid to try to corner the chicken by the Dumpster and the fence. The kid on one side, and me on the other; the chicken had nowhere to go, except up, which it tried.

The kid, quicker than I had imagined, grabbed the chicken by its rough yellow-orange legs. A loud squawk broke the tension. White flapping feathers floated every-where and made me laugh. With his arms wrapped tightly over the large bird, the boy smiled at me. I noticed blood dripping down his arm from where the chicken had scratched him. I studied the color.

"*Muchas gracias*," he said with the slightest nod of his head.

"*De nada*," I responded, and watched as he walked away.

"You want to get me fired?" Delores asked as she shook her head at me.

I didn't. We needed the extra money. Jay stood by the Mart, white haired and red faced. He shook both fists at the figure of the boy who disappeared in the distance.

"Unsanitary beasts," I overheard him say to Delores as they both entered the store. I wasn't sure if he meant the kid or the chicken. Everyone knew how Jay felt about the Mexicans in town.

Who knew how he felt about me? I was both Mexican and white. I lived in the middle, on Allen Street, near the border of the Great Divide.

AVERAGE

I slid back into the Nova and turned the key several times before the rumble of the engine started. I pulled into Jedediah Jr.'s driveway, honked, and stared at the rows and rows of apple trees to the side and behind his house. Sally, his younger sister, pried the blinds open with her fingers and let them fall shut.

I honked again. Sweat beaded up on the back of my legs, making the cotton of the jeans stick. I couldn't remember a hotter June.

Jed raced out of the front door, his unbuttoned shirt as red as his hair was orange. His freckles looked like they were blasted on with spray paint.

"Got a late start today," Jed said as he leaned over to punch me in the arm. "Damn, it's hot." Jed spread his shirt wide and started flapping it wildly to circulate air. If his shirt were a pair of wings, he would've flown away.

The smell of onions and armpits spread throughout the car. "You ever shower?" I asked, laughing.

"Why do you think I was late?" He rubbed his fingers through his hair to show me that it was wet, not greasy.

Jed always had this smell about him, his "love musk," he called it. Before he buttoned up his shirt completely, I saw red marks across his neck and chest. "What happened?" I asked.

"You know Dad," Jed said. "Threw me in a choke hold after I told him to shut up."

"Why can't you be quiet sometimes?"

"I was quiet when he started going on and on about the trees and how they didn't get enough chilling hours. But then he started going on and on about Mama. Then you know how it goes—the good-for-nothing son who prefers to hang out with his good-for-nothing friend instead of taking care of the good-for-nothing family orchard. I'm going to stand up to him one of these days, you'll see."

I wondered why Jed made things worse for himself. I would've just worked in the damn orchard and kept my mouth shut. That's what my father did. He worked hard, even though he never kept a job for long.

I knew Jed was afraid his father would take the money away if he discovered him working at the ranch. And that probably wouldn't be the worst of it. That's what his father did when Sally made money looking after Ms. Gray. Sally cleaned for that old woman, and when she died Ms. Gray left her a necklace. He took that too.

We parked two blocks away from the railroad tracks and

crossed over them as we walked to Fifth Street. Three men stood near the stop sign. Their skin was a dark contrast against their white shirts. They didn't look pleased to see us. Competition. Most of the jobs were available before the sun rose, only some in the later hours. They'd probably been waiting a while.

Jed nodded his head at them and drew out a loud "Howdy." If he wore a hat, he would've tipped it. The men did not look amused. I'm not sure if they spoke English. Me, I just avoided looking into their eyes.

Jedediah sat on the sidewalk and unconsciously ran his hand over his Adam's apple. I made some space between us so I wouldn't be "seduced" by the love musk. I fanned my face with the sucking dry heat of the air and regretted choosing such a dark shirt. I was a signal on the ground, drawing all of the sun's rays into me.

"*Mira!*" one of the men yelled. I looked away from the sky and stared at the approaching car. Border Patrol.

All three men raced into the field.

"Holy crap," Jed said after two officers tore off after them. In the distance, I watched as an officer tackled one of the men to the ground and held a nightstick against the back of his head while the other officer arrested him.

The other two men kept running, but the arrested man was carried to the car. His head clunked against the door frame as the officers shoved him in.

Besides thinking about how much his head must hurt, I wondered what was going on in the man's mind. He turned his head and stared at the field, probably looking for his buddies or wishing he'd been able to run faster.

"Holy crap," Jed said again, as they drove off.

"What do you think will happen to him?" I asked when the Border Patrol car was out of sight.

"Lock him up in jail?" Jed shrugged. "Ship him off somewhere?"

I didn't say anything for a second, thinking of what it would be like for his family waiting for him to return home and wondering what had happened to him when he didn't.

It wasn't right.

"Hey, we should take off. It's probably not safe," I said.

"We're fine," Jed said.

He might've felt fine, but I didn't. I turned around and searched for the two other men one last time, but they were long gone.

Neither Jed nor I said anything else.

After about twenty minutes, a Silverado slowed to a standstill and a cowboy rolled down the passenger window. "Got any experience working on fences?" he asked.

We stood up. The man eyed us through a pair of oversized sunglasses, which he slid down the bridge of his bulbous nose.

Only Jedediah said anything. "Yes, sir." He made a motion toward me.

"You boys old enough to be working?"

"Yes, sir," Jed answered, forcing a Texas accent. I don't know how he kept from laughing.

"Good ol' American boys. Thirty years together between

the two of us. Think it all kind of averages out. We're hard workers. Won't regret it."

"I like the spirit, boy," the man answered. "You two can come with me. Got a job at Darby Guest Ranch."

I didn't know anything about the ranch, but I'd passed by it before.

We climbed into the back of his truck and slid low into the sizzling truck bed. I couldn't stop thinking about what would happen to those men.

Riding in the truck bed, I remembered Loco holding me on his lap when we hitchhiked so I wouldn't tumble out. He sang songs and taught me how to roll the letter *r* on the tip of my tongue. Delores stared at all the land we passed by.

"What are you thinking?" Loco would ask her.

"About my parents."

Sometimes, we weren't the only ones in the truck. Other men and families would ride together to where the fields needed working. Delores would laugh then and smile, especially if the trip involved passing around beer cans or a flask.

JED AND I SAT up when the truck drove under two thick wooden posts holding up a sign that read, "DGR." The ranch reminded me of Camp Mountain Home, a place where my father worked as a cook for a few weeks.

As we climbed out of the truck, the driver came over and introduced himself with a heavy handshake. "Smithson Darby."

"Jedediah Parker, this is Manz." Jed stretched out his

hand. This time he forgot to talk with the accent. I kept my arms tucked against my side.

"I smell something funny," Smithson Darby said, looking directly at me.

"That would be Jed, sir," I said. Smithson Darby laughed. Jed didn't.

"Nice place you got here," Jed said, obviously changing the subject. "Imagine it has a fine history." He'd mastered the art of sucking up, although he didn't have the sense to use it with his father.

"This ranch has been in our family for five generations now. Grandmother Darby came here over a hundred years ago after having to fight Indians and the like. You ain't an Indian, are you, boy?" Mr. Darby asked, looking right at me.

"No, sir. Part Mexican."

"I'll try to forgive you," he said with a pneumonic laugh. I curled my toes in my boots.

"The regular boys here have their hands tied with the summer camp going on. Need a new fence around the ranch. What's standing is rotted and about to fall. I don't care about privacy, but I want a border around the place.

"Keep the same pattern: post, X, post. Tools are in the shed. A pile of mesquite is behind the Big House from when we cleared more land. Get started with the rodeo arena." He took a breath and licked at a spit cake in the corner of his mouth. "Lunch is from noon till one. It's part of your pay."

I watched him as he walked away. His feet swung forward and he slung his shoulders back. I expected him to have holsters on both hips. We weren't even sure how much we were going to get paid. I guess I should've been happy I had a job.

We walked to the shed, and when we opened the door, a trickle of dust spilled out. I placed my shirt over my nose and closed my eyes for a second, suddenly afraid of seeing something awful, like a ghost from one of Grandmother Darby's dead Indians.

Jed laughed. "Nothing to worry about."

How could he be so sure? I opened my left eye first, then my right. Jed placed a hand on a shovel and stared into a barrel of nails. Three crude saws were propped up against the wall along with several large rakes, shovels, and some other gardening tools.

We searched for the tallest building and assumed it was the Big House. A faded Texas flag hung from a pole and a large wooden *Welcome* sign was nailed on the front door.

"Bet this is where Grandma Darby shacked up," Jed said. He slapped his hands together and added squeaky mattress spring noises. I tried not to laugh, but the more I tried, the more I busted up.

Around the building, we saw a massacre of mesquite trees piled high and wide. Most of it was bundled and ready, but a good portion wasn't.

"You know how long this is going to take to get all this crap cleaned up?" Jed asked. "Ain't going to be a one day job."

We spent the rest of the morning hours behind the Big House measuring and splitting up the sturdiest and the largest of the branches. Just as the lunch bell rang, a two-inch thorn pierced my skin. When I pulled the thorn out, my skin itched and burned.

I sucked on my index finger as Jed and I walked to the dining hall. My finger felt hot in my mouth.

A line of folks spilled out of the door. Most of them were kids from the camp. Gabriel would've gone to a place like this.

"Manz, over there."

Ahead, serving the guests in a trough line was a girl with bangs that lay slightly above her wide-set eyes. Egyptian eyes.

"Play it cool," Jed whispered when we were next in line.

"Tea?" Egyptian Eyes asked.

"No ma'am, I'm part Mormon. Can't have it, but I wouldn't mind a little of you sometime."

I literally cringed and I stepped on his foot in an effort to prevent him from saying anything else. Jed lifted it up like a dog with an injured paw and gave me a snarling glare. What Jed lacked in height, he tried to make up in confidence. Egyptian Eyes smiled, her nose and lips triangular.

"No, thanks," she answered. "I'm Catholic and I like 'em quiet." Her eyes stared into mine. I felt my cheeks tingle and then I started to itch.

"Tea?" she asked. I blinked because I wasn't sure I'd seen her lips move.

"Yes," I answered, after a pause. "Please."

"Sweetened or unsweetened?" Her words and the movements of her lips weren't in sync.

"Sweet," I said, and waited again for her to speak so I

could better time the movement of her lips and the sound of her words. Silently, she slid over a glass of water and a glass of sweet tea. "Thanks."

She smiled again and I smelled flowers so strong my nose burned. Like the smell from a mountain laurel, almost like the way a red grape tastes. Jed knocked his knee into the back of my leg so hard it buckled and I almost tipped the tray over. I pictured the tea spilling and splashing all over the floor.

"You smell that?" I asked Jed as we slid our trays down.

"Shut up, already."

Before I had a chance to explain, the floral smell disappeared. "Never mind."

After lunch, we got back to cleaning up the mesquite. The sun was unmercifully hot and my shirt was drenched in sweat. As the sun finally lowered in the sky, Smithson Darby trotted over for inspection. His jeans rode up tightly over his thick waist. The old man's belt buckle protruded like an enormous belly button.

"I expect more work from you tomorrow." He handed us each a twenty-dollar bill. I crumpled it into my hand before sliding it into my pocket. "I'm assuming you boys need a ride back?"

"Yes, sir," Jed said.

Out of his folded sleeve, Smithson Darby pulled a package of cigarettes, which he pointed in our direction. Jed pinched one out of the pack, but I shook my head no. He gave Jed a light.

"I'll pick you boys up at the same time, same place tomorrow?"

Jed nodded and held his cigarette carefully as we climbed into the back of the truck. My muscles adhered to the metal when I sat down.

Jed blew smoke in my direction and laughed when I started hacking. I couldn't say exactly what it was, but there was something different about Jed.

"WHAT CHOICE WOULD YOU have made?" I asked Jed after Delores gave birth to Gabriel.

"I don't know," he said. He surprised me when he asked, "Aren't you somewhat relieved?"

"No," I told him. That's when I first noticed how much had changed between us. Gabriel was going to be Delores and Tom's son—my half-brother. He was my family.

"I'VE NEVER BEEN ABLE to understand you," I told Jed in the back of the truck. "No tea, but you smoke. How Mormon is that?" I managed to ask when I caught my breath.

"Dad is the Mormon and Mama's an atheist, so I figure it all averages out."

"You and your averages."

"You and your sweet tea." Jed reached over and filliped my ear.

I laughed as he flicked the cigarette onto the road. It burst into a red glow that faded immediately.

FOCUS

An alarm blared. I sat up in bed and looked around the room for a moment, wondering where the noise came from. The sheets got tangled around my legs as I stood up to pound my fist on the clock. The ringing only grew more intense, so I ripped the plug out of the wall. The racket lowered to a hum.

But the hum continued and vibrated louder. "Delores!" I yelled. I hid my panic the best I could. "You awake?"

"Yeah," she said. Her voice sounded like it came from Gabriel's room.

"You hear that?"

"Hear what?" she said coming down the hall.

"The alarm!" I knew she could hear the panic.

"It went off for just a second."

"You hear anything now?" Panic spread everywhere inside me. Delores probably heard my panic as loud as I heard the humming.

"What are you talking about?"

"You don't hear *anything*?"

"No. You're worrying me." She must not have heard the noise, or else she couldn't have been so rational.

I took several deep breaths to calm myself down. The alarm was loud enough to wake the dead. Maybe my ears were extra sensitive. "I got dibs on the shower," I said, trying to calm down.

"Good, I can tell you've been hanging around Jed." When she smiled, Delores looked pretty, but I was too nerved up to tell her so.

I stepped into the shower and strained my ears to see if I could still hear the ringing hum. Thankfully, all I heard was the stream of water slapping the tiles.

"No wonder there's a drought in Rockhill," Delores said after I dressed and entered the kitchen. "I need to get to work soon." She opened a bottle of scotch and took a swig to wash down breakfast. I walked out of the room so I wouldn't have to watch her drink.

"Got your keys?"

I slipped the keys out of my pocket and dangled them in front of her. I couldn't look her in the eyes. Delores grabbed her purse. Silently, we got into the old black car. The drive to the Mart would've been quieter if Delores didn't keep clearing her throat. I finally cleared my own out of frustration.

Driving, my mind kept replaying the time Tom and I assembled the crib. We struggled for hours to put the damn thing together. "Grab the Phillips," Tom said.

I walked to the garage. Passing the kitchen, I caught Delores swigging from a bottle.

"Just a taste," she said in confidence. She was ten weeks pregnant. I walked back into the nursery without any tools. But I didn't tell Tom even though I felt like hitting the wall.

"HAVE A GOOD DAY," Delores said as I pulled into the parking lot. Jay Jackson watched us from inside his office. His eyes stared so long and hard I felt guilty even though I hadn't done anything wrong.

Once Delores got out I blared the music loudly so not a soul could hear my thoughts. Some Johnny Cash song.

Jed was waiting on the curb when I picked him up. "Hey, how are you?" I asked as he opened the wide door to the Nova.

"Fine." He slammed the door shut. It didn't catch, so he slammed the door harder. "Dad was in one of his moods."

"Shit."

"Nah, in one of the good moods. Can't remember the last time he's had one of those. He took Mama, Sally, and me to the Crockett County Grill and didn't say anything when I ordered bacon-wrapped shrimp or when Sally ordered sirloin. We had a really good time, laughing and such."

"Good for you." I didn't mean for it to sound so bitter. "What got into your old man?" I'd known Jed for years and his father's good moods were as rare as an apple blossom in January.

Jed shrugged his shoulders.

When we walked across the train tracks, we stood alone

on the corner of Fifth. Those other men might've gotten busted. Either that or they moved on.

"Why don't you just drive to the ranch?" Jed asked after we'd been waiting with no sign of Smithson Darby.

"That isn't the way it works. Besides, all I got is a permit. Promised Delores if I drove alone, it would just be short errands. Don't you ever worry your dad will see you standing here?" I asked, even though I knew Jed's father probably couldn't afford to hire day labor.

"Nah. He don't scare me."

Jed Sr.'s orchard had done quite well for a while. His mom made a bit too, selling apple jams and apple butters. Even though times were tough now, his family had that land and that house, roots in their orchard they could all trace deep down. They didn't know, but in some way, I had roots growing there too.

The Silverado finally turned the corner. I'd had my doubts he was going to show up.

His raspy voice issued from the truck window, "Howdy, boys. Ready to work?"

"Yes, sir," Jed said.

After we settled in the truck, I made sure the windows were closed before I whispered, "Think we might get paid more today?" Didn't want Mr. Darby to hear me.

"Twenty dollars ain't so bad."

"Still saving up for a car?"

"Yeah, but I want to buy a decent Christmas gift for Mama and Sally this year. What about you?"

"I guess I'll buy some things for me and Delores." I thought of the paintbrushes I bought my mother for her birthday. The package sat on the changing table, unopened.

I didn't mention to Jed that I was saving for a trip out of Rockhill. Jed and I talked about running away together shortly after Gabriel died and after Jed's father just about beat the stink out of him for using insecticides during the blooming period.

These days, though, I wanted it to be just me when I left. Jed wanted to go farther west and spit into the Grand Canyon. There was no particular place I wanted to visit. I needed the time alone to get inside my head and work my way back out of it.

"Same old, same old with Delores?"

I nodded. I didn't mention the other night when I heard her in the bathroom. I suppose I was ashamed enough for crying and for starting the fight between us anyway. The thought of the mirror sent a shiver through my skin. I should've made sure I shattered it.

Once we got off the truck, we immediately went to work on the pile of mesquite. As we moved close to it, I heard the hum again, and frantically looked around. The hum vibrated in the pile of wood.

"You hear that? Think there's a rattler in the mesquite?"

It didn't take a second before Jed picked up a handsaw and kicked the mesquite. We hunted for the rattlesnake, and while Jed stopped to catch his breath, I told him it must've been the locusts.

"Must've been," he said, but he jerked his shoulders up like he had a wicked case of the willies.

It took us at least three hours to finish cleaning up the rest of the mesquite. Jed's head rotated nervously from side to side, on the lookout for any snakes. I twitched, more out of fear of hearing the humming again than anything else.

We took a break a few minutes early and waited for the lunch bell to ring. I kept the Big House in view and didn't relax until the bell finally sounded. "You think she'll be there again?"

"Who?"

"Egyptian Eyes?"

Jed laughed and asked if I meant the girl from the day before. He lifted up his arms and sniffed his pits.

"She'll be drowned in your musk."

Jed knocked into me. "Shove it!"

When Egyptian Eyes served us in line, she had a glass of water waiting for Jed, and a glass of tea for me.

"Sweet," she said. I watched her lips and her words; they seemed more synchronized. I noticed a light layer of black fuzz past her sideburns. I wanted to reach out and feel if her face was as soft as it looked.

"Sweet," I repeated, still staring at the hair on her face. "Thanks."

"Why don't you ask her out?" Jed asked when we took a seat with our trays. I stared at a disco ball and the sprays of light emitting from it. It's not that I didn't think about asking her out, it was her answer and what came after that bothered me. I didn't want to invite her into my life and not know where I was taking her.

"You two would make a good match."

I took my eyes off the colors. "Because we're both Mexican?"

"Don't be paranoid, Manz. She just seems to be into you. Besides, you're only half Mexican."

Hearing him say that reminded me of something I'd read. My grandmother wrote us letters that were forwarded, sometimes months later. Delores always searched out the post office as soon as we moved on to the next town. "Will you send pictures of the half-breed?" she asked in one letter.

"A half-breed?" I asked Delores.

"You read my mail!" she said accusingly. "Don't mind her. My mother doesn't mean anything by it."

"Why does she hate me?"

"She doesn't hate you. She's just ignorant and doesn't know any better."

I wasn't sure if Delores sent pictures of me or not. I didn't want to know what my grandparents thought of me. I imagined my grandfather was like Jay Jackson. After he died of cancer, my grandmother's letters came almost daily.

After lunch, Jed and I knocked over rotted fence posts. Mr. Darby ambled over with a tall glass of something in one hand and a cigarette in the other. Sitting in the rodeo bleachers, he spread his legs out in front of him and kicked his boots together.

"Better work today," Mr. Darby said several feet back. He

sucked long and hard on the cigarette, forcing his lips into a wrinkled pucker. I turned my head away before he expelled the smoke. Even though we were outside, I could taste the smoke through my nasal passage.

"It ain't time to leave yet though. You boys got another forty-six minutes," Mr. Darby said, and blew out another plume of smoke. I felt a coughing fit coming on.

Jed and I worked feverishly. We dug out the warped posts, even if they were only slightly rotted. Couldn't have anything left standing that wasn't solid.

THE USUAL AND THE UNUSUAL

The whining of brakes shattered the silence of the house. Even if I'd been asleep, the grinding of the brakes would be loud enough to wake me up. I peeked out the window and saw Tom's truck, minus a trailer, parked on the street. It was him for sure.

I unlocked the front door and walked down the hall to brew the coffee, even though it was after midnight. When Tom was home, the pot never emptied. Sometimes, Tom boiled water and crushed coffee beans over the stove—his trucker version of cowboy coffee.

The burly man reached his arm out to pat me on the back as soon as he came into the kitchen. "Good to see you. Delores sleeping?" Tom groaned and stretched by stepping on the tip of his toes and picking pretend apples from the sky.

"Yeah." I watched as he continued stretching.

"That woman could sleep through a truck crashing into the living room."

We caught each other's eyes for a moment, but didn't say anything. Neither one of us could forget the coma-like state Delores was in after what happened with Gabriel.

"Everything go well?" I asked Tom.

"The usual. What about you?" He stopped his stretching and dug his fingers into his beard.

"The usual." And the unusual. "How can you stand coming back here?"

"That's the thing. Wherever you go, you come back somewhere. Somewhere has always been here for me. It's where my home and family is. Listen to this joke I heard," Tom said as he walked into the kitchen to pour himself a cup of coffee. I grabbed a cup from the dish strainer for myself.

"So a blonde just bought herself a new yellow Corvette and went out for a drive, and she cut off a trucker," Tom said, already starting to laugh. "The trucker told her to pull over and when she did, he got a piece of chalk and drew a circle on the road. 'Stand in the circle and don't move,' the trucker warned. Then he went to the car and tore up her leather seats. When he looked at her she was smiling, so he said, 'You think that's funny?' Then he grabbed a bat and smashed all the windows.

"But when he saw the blonde again, she was still smiling. This ticked off the trucker even more and he sliced her tires. She started laughing and the trucker was about to lose it. So he set her 'Vette on fire. The blonde started

31

laughing so hard she was about to fall down. "'What's so funny now?'

"She answered, 'When you weren't looking, I stepped outside the circle four times.'"

Tom laughed so hard he held a hand over his stomach. I forced an appreciative chuckle, and then sipped the coffee. The warm liquid sank down my throat. It was good to hear Tom laugh. There was a long span of time when he didn't tell any of his jokes.

"Good one, huh?" Tom opened the fridge and grabbed a block of cheddar and some lunchmeat. "Hungry?"

"No," I said, but I stayed in the kitchen with him while he made a sandwich. It was gone in three bites.

"Night, Manz." Tom brought his plate and coffee mug to the sink. "I'm so tired I'm starting to feel nuts."

"I know that feeling. Night, Tom."

WHEN I WALKED INTO the living room the next morning, Delores shoved something in the cabinet. The clinking of a bottle gave her away. "Morning," she said.

"Same to you."

I watched as she filed Tom's letters. He'd write them all out the night before he left for his trips and pile them on the table. Sometimes, Delores would rip them open before his truck left the driveway. Then she'd reread the letters and dig out the old ones. She kept Tom's letters in the same place she filed her mothers'.

I used to sneak a peek at them all. In some letters, Tom

wrote jokes like the ones he loved to tell. In others, he'd write about their special dates. Many of the letters mentioned his excitement for Gabriel, of having a son together. At the end of every letter, Tom told Delores to say hi to me.

"YOU GOING TO GET ready for work?" I asked Delores. The coffeepot gurgled as hot liquid flowed out.

"Mr. Jackson gave me the day off. Be nice to spend some time with Tom." She dipped a glass into the sink. It immediately drowned in a thick foam of bubbles.

"Do you mind if I take the car out?"

"You going far?" She pulled the glass out of the suds and scrubbed it with a washcloth.

"Just to Jed's—it's too hot out there to walk." I hadn't mentioned anything to her about the job at the ranch. She wouldn't have cared though—she was pregnant at my age and had more responsibility than working on a fence.

"Fine. Just don't cause any trouble."

WHEN JED GOT INTO the car, I saw Sally looking through the blinds. She waved us goodbye. I waved back to her, but I wasn't sure if she saw me.

"Top o' the mornin'." Jed greeted me with his phoniest Irish accent. I was glad to see Jed upbeat and bruise-free.

Smithson Darby arrived on time, and when we drove under the posts, I swore it said "OWR." But as we passed under and I looked from the other side, it read "DGR," like always. I shook my head.

"You boys get as much done as yesterday and we'll all be happy campers," Smithson Darby said.

Jed rolled his eyes as we walked toward the Big House. Mr. Darby went inside the old home and the *Welcome* sign flapped against the door after he shut it. We went behind the house to cut up more of the mesquite.

Even with the cuts on my hands, they would never be as calloused or as overworked as my father's. Delores used to rub cream on his hands every night, but it didn't change their leathery feel.

Like some kind of vision, Egyptian Eyes walked toward us with glasses of water in her hands. I hadn't realized we'd been working for three hours.

She wore a sleeveless shirt and her arms were so muscular that she looked like a Greek athlete. The black hairs of her arms contrasted with her dark skin. "Papa Darby said you boys had been working hard."

"Papa Darby?" Jed asked. His eyebrows lifted so high I thought they were going to come right off his face. He started laughing hysterically.

"All the girls at the ranch call him that. He's like a grandpa." This time, her words and her lip motions were synchronized for sure. She handed us each a glass of water, which we chugged in an instant. She stood there, swaying her arms back and forth. I watched the lines of her muscles stretch and retract.

"Thanks. You like it here?" I asked. I couldn't quite look her in the eyes, so I focused on the back-and-forth motion of her arms. My cheeks glowed red when I thought about the hairs all over her body.

"It's not so bad. Only place I could find work this summer. Not many jobs in Herman."

"I'll get a different saw," Jed said, excusing himself from our conversation. "Don't worry, I'll take my time," he whispered to me, but he was loud enough for us both to hear.

"Does he always smell like that?"

I laughed. "Yeah. You get kind of used to it."

She asked where I lived and when I answered "Rockhill," I stretched my arms out and studied my own hair and muscles. My hair and skin weren't as dark.

"That place is even worse than Herman. You think things would change. Even when they do, it doesn't seem like anything is different, really. Ever feel that way?"

"Sure," I said, not quite understanding what change she talked about. I kept quiet though. I couldn't put into words what I felt. A long pause filled our conversation.

"I'm Vanessa Ortiz, by the way." She held out her hand, which was large and calloused like mine should've been. I think I preferred Egyptian Eyes to Vanessa.

"Isaiah Martinez," I said with my hand extended. My ears tingled again hearing my given name. "I don't go by Isaiah though. Everyone calls me Manz."

"You the Manz, eh?" she said in a tough-guy accent. I pictured what she would look like flexing her arms.

I smiled at her. "Manz as in *manzana*."

"Apple?"

"My father said my cheeks looked like apples when I was a baby." I didn't tell her that he and Delores had been drinking when the nickname came about.

Vanessa reached over and rubbed my cheek lightly, just the way I wanted to touch hers. My ears weren't the only things tingling.

"So does your dad still agree?"

I crunched on an ice cube I fished out of the glass. "He's dead."

"I'm sorry," Vanessa said, but to my relief, she didn't ask how. "I'll see you at lunch." She stared ahead, so I looked over and saw Jed walking up the hill with a different saw. She pulled her dark hair behind her ears.

"It was nice talking to you," I said, before she started walking away. I watched as Jed gave her a nod.

"You ask her out?"

"Not yet. I probably scared her off. Things like this take time."

"That's one tough girl. Don't know what you're waiting for."

The thing that really took time was cutting up the mesquite. I wasn't sure why we were using the mesquite to build such a crappy fence. Jed wiped the sweat beads from his forehead and I was sweating buckets when the lunch bell rang.

Vanessa smiled over at us while we waited in line. When she slid my tea over, she slipped me a folded yellow note. When I opened it up, I traced my fingers over her phone number.

"Thanks," I said, hoping I didn't make too much of an ass out of myself. This seemed next to impossible.

"Score," Jed said when we got to the end of the line.

Before leaving the hall, I hunted down a pen and scrawled my number on a napkin. While Vanessa waited on someone, I slipped it to her.

"You the Manz," Jed said. Somehow, he must've overheard our conversation. I looked at him, but he seemed too calm for this to be one of his jokes.

Still wondering how Jed could've been listening in, I went back to work. My father used to say he hoped I never knew what hard work was. I guess hard work was the only way I could know Loco now.

My shoulders ached from all the sawing, so I straightened up and stretched. When I turned my neck, a sensation of hyperreality swallowed me. The cloudless sky throbbed blue. Almost like the blue of Delores's painting.

In the background, children laughed and their voices jumbled together as they rode horses near the corral. I heard a horse a great distance away whinny. When I looked across the ranch, I studied a section of the fence. Warped, it stood: post, X, post. The crossing pieces of wood created four triangles. The triangles pulsed just like the sky. The wings of a monarch flapped as it fluttered by.

"What are you staring at?" Jed asked. I closed my eyes for a moment. When I opened them, things seemed . . . a little less real.

"Trying to stay focused." He didn't know how hard it was

to stay focused. "You think they're trying to poison us in the dining hall?"

"Manz, you crack me up. You think Cleopatra put you on a hit list? Why'd she poison you when those big hands could just strangle you?"

I shrugged.

Getting back to the job, I kept looking around, waiting for the pulsing sensation to consume me again. "You notice anything weird?" I asked Jed about an hour later to be on the safe side.

"Just you."

Finally the sun lowered in the sky and Smithson Darby handed us each another twenty-spot and told us to knock off for the day.

In the back of Darby's truck, Jed sneezed, then crossed his arms underneath his head and stared into the sky. It no longer glowed the color of Gabriel's room.

"Do you see shapes in things?" I glanced at the truck window to make sure nobody overheard me.

"What you talking about?" Jed turned and looked at me. I could almost see my reflection in his pupils.

"I don't know, like seeing a certain shape over and over again."

"You're really starting to get weird, you know that? You make too much out of things."

I closed my eyes and hoped that's what it was.

FOOTSTEPS

T om placed the phone receiver down and ran his
fingers through his beard.

"You going to take the load?" I asked. When I was
younger, I hated the sound of the phone ringing because
it meant another job offer. I liked having Tom around.
Delores drank less with him there and he always had his
jokes or stories to tell.

When we first moved into his house, I trusted him, even if
I didn't exactly like him. I hated the situation. I didn't want
to grow roots. Didn't want to grow up weak like the apple
trees with the blight. I wanted to stay on the move, the way
Delores, Loco, and Manz did things. But still, I trusted Tom.
When my father died, everything came apart. Tom offered
tape, even though I knew there wouldn't be glue.

"What'd you ask, Manz? Do I have to take a dump?" Tom
laughed and he placed his hand over his stomach like he

was trying to keep his insides in place. "Got to find the humor in everything." He took his thumb and index finger and traced the length of his beard.

He didn't always find the humor in everything. I remember Tom crying after he found out what was wrong with his real son.

"No, to answer your question, the offer wasn't good enough," Tom said. "Seems like the Man is out to get you these days."

Loco said that all the time. I heard his voice. "The Man is coming. The Man is out for us. Be careful of the Man." I used to wonder who the Man was and what he looked like. Loco must've known. One of the things I remembered about my father was that he always looked over his shoulder. *Loco*. Crazy.

"No, this job had multiple pickups and they expected me to lump."

"Like a lump in your drawers?" I asked.

Tom started laughing, but not so hard he had to hold his guts in place.

"That's the way, son. Always got to find the humor," Tom said, pausing to allow a chuckle. "Lumping means you gotta unload the freight yourself. Did I ever tell you about the boxes?"

Without even waiting for a response, Tom poured himself a cup of coffee. "So I was carrying close to six hundred boxes in the trailer. Six hundred boxes, can you imagine? I started unloading them all. Five hours later, I was still lugging out those damn things. Now I leave the lumping to the shipper—it's his responsibility anyway. He don't help me drive my truck. I don't help him with his freight. Ever think about driving a truck?"

Again, he didn't wait for me to respond. "As soon as my legs were long enough, Father taught me to drive. He left me the truck and I knew what I had to do."

Driving a truck was better than waiting around for odd jobs to open. Seemed like everyone got lost in the footsteps of those who came before them. I didn't know where I was stepping.

Delores had made it clear she was worried I wouldn't find a good job someday.

"Father used to take me on trips with him. I don't know. It just seemed to fit. You should be my second seat driver sometime, Manz. You could learn how to do all the paperwork—fuel receipts, permits, the logbook . . . "

"Sounds interesting. Look, Tom, Jed's probably waiting on me."

"I get it," Tom said, and swirled around the coffee in the mug before taking a sip.

"See you soon," I said, even though I wasn't sure I would.

JED WASN'T WAITING ON the curb, so I blasted the horn. I cleaned the dirt underneath my fingernails while I waited, but then I grew nervous because Jed didn't usually make me wait that long. I held the horn down with my fist. Everything felt too calm. Too silent. Sally wasn't standing near the blinds.

I raced out of the car. My heart pumped so fast I was sure it would explode. Jed's in there, dead on the floor, I thought. I knew he was dead. His old man had finally killed him.

"The Man is going to get you," a voice said, almost as if it was above me. It reminded me of my father's voice. Good Lord, I hoped it wasn't too late. "The Man is going to get you." Loco? A shiver raced through my body as I pushed through the door, grateful it wasn't dead bolted, the way I kept mine locked. Jed's voice boomed from the living room.

"You don't keep secrets in this family!" he screamed. He was alive, and so angry I don't think he noticed me.

Sally stood in front of him, her feet shoulder width apart. "You'll find out soon enough."

"If you don't tell me, I'm going to make you sorry!"

Sally continued to stand in front of him, but this time, she said nothing. With the palm of his hand, Jed jammed it against his sister's throat and shoved her into the wall. She stood stiff with fear. She looked blue.

"Damn it! Tell me!"

I bolted into the room and grabbed his shoulders, throwing him off of Sally. I bashed him in the nose.

"You're no better than your old man!" Just as I raised my fist to smash his face again, Sally pulled at my elbow.

"Enough," she said. Her voice crackled as she massaged her throat. She pulsed with the color blue.

"Why'd you do that?" Jed asked while trying to stop the blood rushing from his nose.

"You're just like him!"

"He's going to kill me if I get blood on the carpet." Jed pulled himself off the ground, and when he staggered too close to Sally, she jumped back.

"If you do anything like this again, I'll be the one to kill you." I heard my voice, and I knew it was me talking, but it didn't feel like me. "Promise you'll leave her alone."

"She better watch it. No secret is worth keeping," he said, keeping Sally in view.

I knocked my shoulder into Jed and walked away.

"Where you going?"

"Got a job to do." Sally didn't deserve to be treated that way. She'd always been there for me. For Jed too. I walked toward the front door, still wide open. My legs shook. I wondered how many people saw what happened. How many people knew what happened in that house and didn't say? How many people who lived in that house and didn't say?

"Not without me. Sally is my sister. . . ."

"You better promise, Jed." My temples throbbed.

"Fine, I promise. Who cares about her damn secret anyway?"

Sally looked like a blue deer frozen in the headlights of a truck heading down Highway 90.

When I got into the car, Jed opened the passenger side. "What the hell was that about?" I asked him. The sound of my voice felt detached from my body.

"She overheard Dad and Mama arguing, but she wouldn't tell me about what. I don't know, the more she refused to tell me anything, the more I . . . I lost it."

The thoughts in my head were too loud. Everything was too noisy. The whispering of voices, a louder voice saying something—the crunching of footsteps.

While we waited for Smithson Darby, Jed told me he'd use the day's money to buy her a gift. I could just barely understand him.

The noise was too loud for me to answer. "Quiet!" I yelled.

CALLS

"Manz, that you?" Delores said into the phone. Her voice echoed like she was in some kind of chamber.

"Yeah." I swirled the magenta and the black paint, still disappointed I couldn't replicate the color of blood. I never painted anything, just blended colors together on white paper to watch the changes take place.

"You all right? Listen, we'll talk later. Joanne is giving me a ride home tonight. I'll be in late, so don't worry about me. Make yourself some dinner."

"Thanks," I said. I thought of her reaction if she found me in Gabriel's room, using her paint. She never noticed the supplies I used.

Delores bumped into me one day as I passed her in the hall. She stepped closer to the bathroom to pretend she'd been in there and not in the baby's room. She couldn't walk a straight line.

"Why aren't you painting?" I asked her. I wanted her to be happy and to have something other than drinking.

"People ask too many questions," she told me. "It's none of their freaking business."

I GOT BACK TO mixing the paint, trying to ignore the humming, whispering, and crunching noises that I wasn't completely sure I was hearing. Paint dripped from the brush. I wondered if Jay Jackson had tapped the phone. He was probably in his office listening to everything. That's most likely why he ran the Mart—to keep track of all the people in town.

I cleaned up and turned on the TV.

Tom left early that morning. Even on Sundays, he worked. But that was his profession, and, as Delores said, his lifestyle.

Years back, Tom had begged Delores to marry him.

"I can't," she said.

"You couldn't marry a stupid truck driver?" he asked. He tried to make it sound like he was joking, but to me it sounded like the start of an argument. "It takes smarts to drive lots of gears, to survive when your brakes go out, to know the handbooks and regulations . . . "

"No," she interrupted. "It isn't that."

"Why not?"

"I can't," Delores told him again. "I just can't."

Secretly, I felt pleased she was loyal to Loco. They'd had rough times, I knew. But they disrupted their lives for each other. Loco was her husband. My father.

Tom quit pressing her, and I didn't give it any more thought until Delores announced she was pregnant. Jed asked if I was angry, but I wasn't; I felt something so deep—excitement, pride, I don't know.

Tom and Delores couldn't stop talking about their baby. They decorated the nursery together. Delores surprised me when she painted the room blue. "I don't care if it's a girl or a boy," she said, "blue is your favorite color."

Tom rubbed her feet and her back. He'd lean over to kiss her stomach and whisper his corny jokes. I don't know how he couldn't smell her breath.

At the time, I didn't know Gabriel had anencephaly. Not even when Delores held my hand over her stomach and I felt the baby. None of us knew. Gabriel was developing without part of his skull and brain.

A NEWS REPORT SHOWED footage of an illegal immigrant raid at a poultry plant in south Texas. The employees were wearing tan smocks and cutting chicken one minute, then handcuffed the next. "We've arrested thirty-nine Mexican nationals and they will be charged for violating immigration laws and document fraud," an INS agent said.

A worker at the plant was interviewed. "It's an injustice. No human being should be considered illegal," she said, wiping her tears. "These people were part of our community until Immigration swept in, and now they're gone. How can any of us feel safe?"

I shook my head, and thought of the bust Jed and I had witnessed. I turned the TV off. I couldn't watch anymore. Right as I walked into the kitchen, the phone rang again.

"Change your mind, Delores?" I asked when I picked it up.

"Excuse me?" a girl asked. She sounded familiar.

I heard myself ask who it was while I dug my thumbnail into my skin.

"Vanessa."

My hand immediately turned sweaty and I tightened my grip around the phone.

"I was hoping you would call. But since you didn't, I, uh, just wanted to. Call, you know?"

My voice softened. "I'm glad you did."

"You have a girlfriend? Delores?"

I didn't speak for a moment, still in shock that Egyptian Eyes Cleopatra Vanessa would call me, Isaiah Luis "Manz" Martinez.

"Listen, I don't mean to be rude, I know it's not any of my business. . . ."

"No, it isn't like that at all. Delores is my mother. She doesn't like going by Mom or anything like that."

Vanessa laughed. "You're kidding. I still call my mom Mamá and kiss her on the cheek like I did when I was a kid."

"And how old are you now?" I asked, then worried it might seem inappropriate. I pulled a piece of skin away from my finger. The air stung the raw skin underneath.

"Sixteen. And you?"

"Sixteen, well, in October."

"You're only fifteen?" she asked. "You seem older." Nervousness rattled in her voice. "My little sister, Wilnelia, is having a *Quinceaños* soon."

I asked her what that was before I rubbed the sweat from my hands onto the quilt.

"You've never heard of a *Quinceañera* before? Wilnelia will be fifteen and is having a party to celebrate; sort of like a Sweet Sixteen. Don't you have any sisters or cousins?"

"No," I said. My mind flashed to Sally. She was fourteen, but who knew how sweet her sixteenth would be.

"Her party will be huge. You should come."

"Yeah. Maybe." I inspected my hands for any other skin to pull at. I tried thinking of other things to say, but nothing came to mind. Vanessa must've sensed how uncomfortable I was because she told me that she'd look forward to seeing me at the ranch.

"Sure." I held onto the receiver long after her goodbye, just wondering if our conversation had been real. The phone beeped a disconnected beep, but I heard something hum and scuttle.

"Who's there?" I called out, listening to the scuttling sound, which grew louder. I thought about the detained poultry workers and ran to the door to make sure it was locked. *The Man is going to get you.*

The scuttling drew nearer, so I rushed to the window. I

paused for a moment, wondering if I really wanted to get closer. I pulled the curtain back and watched a shadowy figure run down Allen Street.

"Get away from here!" I yelled. My throat burned. The shadow looked back at me with a triangular face. I drew the curtains closed.

I turned off all the lights and crawled under the layers of bedding to hide. I burned hot underneath the quilt and sheets, but I was too scared to move. I tried convincing myself to fall asleep, but I was far from that state.

Sheer panic gripped me when I heard the twisting of a key in a lock a couple of hours later.

"Manz, you okay?"

In the dark, I saw Delores. She flipped on a few light switches and staggered into my room. My nerves had liquefied my muscles.

"Is anyone outside?"

"No, the coast is clear." She looked over her shoulder as if she didn't believe what she said. How could she ask if I was okay when she was so far from okay herself?

"Are you sure? Nobody's out there?" I wanted to ask her to check outside again. "I think someone is after me."

"You need help," she said, then hiccupped. When she held her hand over her mouth, I heard plastic rustle.

"No one is out to get you." She set a package of candy circus peanuts on my bed. The orange sugary shapes used to be my favorite.

"To cheer you up." Delores sighed and tapped the bag. I

noticed she had a grease burn on her hand. "They're kind of stuck together. These summer days are getting hotter and hotter." She hiccupped again. "You going to be okay?"

I shrugged.

TALKING

The Nova's engine churned loudly, almost drowning out the noise of my thoughts, but not quite. I felt unsure about seeing Jed. Seemed like we'd been through worse. But witnessing Jed attack Sally like that got to me. Like he was morphing into his old man, forgetting what it was like on the other side.

Was I morphing into my old man?

Jed wasn't waiting when I pulled up, but I didn't want to get out of the car. I didn't want to think of the things that might've been happening. Didn't want to see Sally's eyes staring through the blinds, didn't want to see Sally's eyes reflecting the glow from some kind of headlights. I wanted to know Sally's secret, but a part of me didn't. I needed one less thing to worry about. I placed my hand on the horn and gave it a steady honk.

Jed and I were never perfect kids, never perfect at school,

never the shining apples of Rockhill. When we first came here, Delores and Loco rented a place from a guy called Tío. It wasn't a nice place, but it wasn't bad either. It had a bed and hot water. My father worked for Jedediah Sr., so I got to know Jed Jr. when I followed my father in the orchard.

Tío evicted us not too long after my father died, probably because authorities were involved and he figured Delores wouldn't pay the rent. And it was Tío's car that Loco wrecked.

Jed Sr. tried to get his son to promise he wouldn't hang around with lowlife scum like me. But Jed never made a promise he couldn't keep.

I suppose Jed's father could see that Jed and I equaled trouble. Even the judge said as much when Jed and I were each sentenced with a Class C misdemeanor and had to complete thirty hours of community service for criminal mischief.

I STARED INTO THE orchard full of trees standing so still they seemed petrified. I didn't even notice when Jed flipped the handle of the door. I jumped back, then reached over to unlock it.

"Morning," Jed said after he slid into the seat. His stink followed him.

"Hey, listen, Jed, I think someone was trying to break in last night." I was about to ask if he thought it was a Border Patrol agent, but I didn't. Maybe he was cooperating with them. "Do you think someone would have it out for me?"

"I don't know what you're talking about." He stretched

53

the seatbelt over himself and snapped it into place.

"I just don't understand. Someone is after me."

"I don't understand either." Jed itched at his scalp and flicked something from his fingernail. "Want the rifle?"

I remembered Jed showing it to me before, after his grandfather took him hunting for mule deer. The thought of having a gun in the house didn't make me feel any safer. "No, not for now."

"I wanted to explain to you, about the other day. . . ."

"We already talked about it. Isn't it time for you to switch deodorants?"

"Just like you to not deal with things. Sorry. I guess that's all I can say. So take it or leave it." Jed held his blistered hand out to me, which I shook. His grip startled me.

WHEN WE GOT TO the ranch, Jed and I grabbed the tools we needed. Using our body weight, we dug out the remaining old posts. In their place, we sunk the thickest of the mesquite a third of the way into the ground and packed some gravel and reddish brown dirt around it.

"We're never going to finish this," I said as we headed to the dining hall for lunch. I grew nervous at the thought of seeing Vanessa, or maybe it was even the thought of not seeing her.

"The money isn't that bad. I bought some books for Sally," Jed said.

"You owe her a damn library."

When Vanessa waved at me, I flushed with both anxiety

and relief. I kept my head down, and focused my eyes on the napkin-wrapped silverware and brown tray. Somebody had scratched the initials G.W. into the tray. Even as I walked to the end of the line, I kept my head down. I would hate for her to look at me and see just how interested in her I was.

"Good to see you," she said.

"Likewise," Jed answered.

I looked up. I should've been the first to say something. I refused to say anything second, so I smiled at her. We slid down the rest of the trough, filling our plate with sandwich bread, chopped meat, sliced onions, and pickles. Before we sat down, Jed shoved a piece of bread into his mouth.

"I'm so starved I feel sick," he said. A white chunk flew out of his mouth, but he didn't notice.

"Maybe you shouldn't eat any onions," I said. I stirred the meat around, scooped it into the bread, and decorated it with some pickles. Some kids laughed in the dining hall. When I looked up, all of them stared at me. They burst into laughter.

"Did I do something?" I asked Jed.

"What?" He licked the barbeque sauce off his fingers before building a second sandwich.

"Those kids over there—I know they're laughing at me. You sure I'm fine?"

"I don't know about fine, but I don't see anything. Nobody is looking in our direction. Ignore them; they're just kids." Jed started laughing.

"What the hell?" I asked.

"Remember that time I got caught in grade school drawing on my desk? It was just the outline of a lady. Mrs. Lynn was shocked."

Jed's laughter reminded me of a pendulum swinging. His giddiness and the memory made me laugh too.

"She had me get up in front of the class to apologize for destroying school property and I couldn't get any words out."

"'Cause we were all trying to see your picture," I said. I remembered how Mrs. Lynn had tried covering up Jed's outline with a ruler. It didn't hide much.

"Then you started laughing so hard Mrs. Lynn sent you out of the room," Jed said. "I don't think I've ever heard you laugh so hard. The whole school could hear you busting up in the hall." Jed wiped the tears from his eyes and I coughed to clear the laughter from my throat.

Jed stopped and looked up. "Hey."

"Hey," said Vanessa. She swiveled a chair and sat at our table. "What's so funny?"

"Old school memories," Jed said.

"I got to get back to work soon, but I wanted to see what you were laughing about and say hi."

"Well, hi," Jed said.

"See you later," Vanessa said as she stood up. Before she left, her eyes caught mine. She extended her pinky and her thumb. Holding them up to her ear, she mouthed the words, "Call me."

"Did I miss something?" Jed asked as we put our trays and

dirty dishes up. We didn't leave much trash on our plates, except for the onions Jed didn't eat. Before I walked outside I looked over at the kids. The group wasn't laughing anymore, but they stared at me again, pointing their fingers at me. I lunged forward at them to show them I wasn't afraid.

Jed handed me a toothpick. "So what's the deal?"

"Those kids. You think they're in on something?"

"What are you talking about? I was talking about this." Jed slipped the toothpick into his pocket and held an imaginary phone up to his ear.

"Oh, that. I talked to her the other night. Not a big deal."

"What are you talking about? That's huge!"

"It might be something." Something that horrified and excited me at the same time.

MEMORIES

I ignored the humming sounds by focusing on the setting sun as I drove to pick up Delores. Wild streaks of red, orange, and yellow were washed out by massive thunderheads. It looked nothing like the sunset in Delores's painting. A loud crack of thunder rattled the house. I used to be afraid of storms, of their fury and destruction.

When I was six, we were stranded at Camp Mountain Home. Loco worked as a temporary cook for a few weeks and Delores helped him out in the kitchen. It was a boy's camp, and I had a chance to do things real kids did. I rode my first horse ever and when I was near the corral, I saw a pair of armadillos.

But a week after we were there, a loud crack of thunder shook the camp. The pounding of the rain and the booming of thunder continued throughout the days and nights. The creek water rose over the road; there was no way to get into

Camp Mountain Home and no way to get out.

"Why is God mad at us?" I asked my parents when we were in our room. I winced each time a crack of thunder rumbled overhead.

"God's not angry," Loco said after he took a long drink from his mug. "He's bowling." A loud clap of thunder boomed and I thought of God holding a bowling ball in His hand.

The people that ran the camp set up an emergency shelter in the dining hall. Loco and Delores did what they always did—went about surviving.

After that, I got some of the campers to play "Guess What God's Doing Now." Some kids guessed He was playing drums. Some thought maybe He was running and jumping from cloud to cloud. Others guessed He was playing foursquare.

When my father died, I wondered if he ever bowled with God, even though I was old enough to know otherwise.

WHEN I PULLED INTO the Mart, folks scurried around like a tornado was about to touch down. Maybe something else was about to take place, and I didn't know it.

When Delores saw the Nova, she walked out of the cramped building and stared up into the sky. I wondered if she guessed what God might've been doing. Or where Loco was.

"Looks like rain," she said. "We could sure use it." Delores dabbed raindrops off of her face and pulled her hair out of a ponytail holder. Even though nothing actually tied it back, her hair stayed in the same position.

I peered into the Mart to get a closer look at Jay Jackson.

Before Delores went back to work there, Jed and I used to walk to the Mart all the time to buy a soda or candy. I never bought circus peanuts; I saved those only for special occasions, and even then, I wanted Delores to buy them for me. I think that's why I liked them.

Walking home from school one day, Jed and I saw Jay spying out at us through the cracked door of his office. Just as I'd guessed what God did when it stormed, Jed and I used to guess what Jay did in that room. I used to think he went in there to sleep since he was so old. Jed thought maybe he had a first-class stash of mags in the office. We dared each other to bust through the door to see for sure, but we weren't brave enough until one night when I camped out at Jed's place. Everyone in his family had gone to sleep, even Sally.

"I dare you to find out what that old man does in his room," Jed said.

"Now?" The Mart was closed and my feet weren't up for another walk.

"Are you chicken?" Jed asked.

"No," I said, and accepted the dare.

It was well after midnight when we got to the Mart. The sky was so dark I wondered if my eyes were ever going to adjust. The stars hid behind the clouds.

We tried walking through the front doors of the store, but they were locked with a chain wrapped around the handles. We laughed for even trying. Jed and I slithered around the side of the building and found a window that led to the office. It was high up, so Jed stood on my shoulders and tried to pry it open. Of course it was locked tight too.

We scooped up gravel and pelted it at the window. I knew it wasn't going to do anything, but I threw a handful anyway. Before we had a chance to do any damage, a red-faced Jay Jackson came barreling out near the service station—we learned that's where he lives.

"Stop or I'll kill you!" The shotgun in his hands told us he was serious. "The sheriff is on his way!"

Jay Jackson was no liar. The sheriff arrived and had to pry the shotgun away from Jackson because he was too insistent at aiming the barrel at us.

Jed and I were sentenced with community service cleaning urinals after school at Rockhill High. Delores didn't believe me when I told her I wasn't trying to steal anything. Jed's parents didn't do any asking and he didn't get to do any telling—his father went straight for the belt, armed and ready to set his son straight.

Jed and I never did find out what was in the room. I thought it was practically a miracle Jay offered Delores her job back after all of that business. Maybe he saw her paintings or maybe he forgot I was her son.

AT HOME, I WARMED up tortillas in a pan and Delores and I dipped them in melted butter. The thunder rattled the windowpanes following the flashes of lightning.

"Slightly better than saltine crackers," Delores said as she downed another bite. For a short spell after Loco died, all Delores and I had to eat was a box of crackers. Everything tasted better than those crackers. "Who is Vanessa?"

I literally spat a wad of tortilla out of my mouth. Delores must've had people spying on me. "How do you know about her?" I felt myself growing sick with the thought of all I needed to hide.

"So who is she?" Delores asked again, her attention turning from the buttery tortillas to me, the son whose mind was transparent.

"How do you know about Vanessa?"

"Mothers just know these things," Delores said, and grinned. "Oh, stop looking so freaked out." She pointed at the back of my hand.

I looked at my own hand. How could I have been so stupid? When I got home, I scribbled her name between my thumb and index finger so I'd remember to call. "She's nobody."

Delores didn't seem convinced—she smiled her young smile. I was about to argue with her, but I smiled back. What emotions I had I couldn't seem to control.

"And there is my evidence." My mother smiled again. "Girlfriend?"

I shrugged my shoulders. "Friends." I was hoping for more, but wasn't going to tell her that.

"I was a little younger than you when I met Andres." This was Andres "Loco" Martinez, my father. "I couldn't speak his name without smiling either." Delores looked across the living room like she was searching for him.

She had this apprehensive look on her face like she'd find him all stretched out on the couch, weaving his fingers together, which is something he always did. She'd told this story lots of times when she was drunk, but this time, I didn't stop her.

Delores stuck her finger in a soggy portion of the tortilla. "I used to beg him to say my name over and over again to hear words roll out of his mouth, and I used to say his name over and over in my head. He wanted me to move with him right away, but I was too afraid.

"When I got pregnant, Daddy begged me to make a different decision. What kind of idiot would I be to have a child with a Mexican? Said I was a fool to marry him. What bigger idiot would I be to marry an illegal who just wanted to become a citizen the easy way?" Delores stopped talking and stared down at her plate. "My mom said she'd always love me, but she couldn't go against my father."

I ripped the rest of my tortilla into strips and then into crumbs.

"Loco and I waited until I was eighteen to get officially married, for fear of needing any kind of contact with them."

"When you left, did you ever think about going home?" I'd never asked her that before. I wasn't sure if I'd think about going home, but I knew I'd wonder how everyone was and what they were doing.

"'Wherever you go, you come back somewhere,'" Delores said, quoting Tom. She looked up at me and laughed. "Well, anyway, somewhere was never back with my folks. I never wanted to see them again, not even my mother. They never saw their grandbaby. We made enough sacrifices and had enough complications. Your father had no contact with his family; I left mine."

I was a part of their family, sometimes a stranger in the equation, but a part of it nonetheless. "How did you know you loved him?"

"Are you and that girl, what's her name, Vanessa, serious?"

I shook my head. Delores flicked the flour mush off of her fingernail and chugged a sip of beer. "I didn't want to be without him. I couldn't be without him really. He was sick and I knew he needed me too."

I guess I don't remember my father being sick. I just remember how he sat for hours in the same position, without twitching any body parts. "Are you and Tom going to start trying again?"

Her eyes seemed to ask, *trying for what?* Then she realized what I was asking. "I don't know." Delores gulped the rest of her beer down. "Enough memories." She stood up and went into the bathroom. "Goodnight."

With the lights burning in the living room, I thought about Delores, my age and stuck with all those burdens. I also thought of Tom's face when he told me that one of Delores's tests came back high. Delores never said anything to me after her checkup.

"What does it mean?" I asked Tom.

"She's either having twins or something is wrong with the baby."

I knew that it probably wasn't twins. After the emergency ultrasound, the doctors found out they were having a boy, but also that there was something wrong with him.

Tom and Delores were given a choice between inducing labor or carrying the baby to full-term. The outcome would be the same either way—the baby couldn't live without a functioning brain. I had nightmares thinking about a baby with something so wrong.

Four days later, Delores delivered Gabriel Thomas Henton. He was stillborn and weighed less than a pound.

I felt like I was going to pass out while waiting in the hospital. I had my chance to see the baby, but I couldn't.

"He was perfect," Tom said to me after. "Unless you saw his head, you wouldn't have known."

He broke down then and I couldn't control myself either. Since Delores was two days short of twenty weeks along, the hospital took care of his cremation. They gave us his ashes in a round marble box.

WHEN DELORES CAME OUT of the bathroom, she immediately went to bed. I watched the lightning show for a few more moments in the kitchen before washing the dishes. The clouds were dark and ominous, but I was certain it wasn't going to rain. At least it wouldn't be so hot working at the ranch.

I sighed loudly and dreaded the still of the night.

FRIEND OR FOE

The alarm screeched. I jolted out of bed to turn it off, but it was too early for my alarm to sound. I plugged my ears and searched for the source of the noise. The kitchen light glowed.

"Who's there?" I yelled above the ringing, but it was too loud to hear my own voice. I crept into the kitchen, and to my relief, Delores was sitting at the table. The stovetop burned a bright red beneath a teakettle whistling with steam.

"Didn't you hear that?" I asked her as I flipped the switch on the stove off. She seemed unaffected by it all. "Delores?" Seeing her brought back a memory of Loco. Alive on the inside, but seemingly dead to the world. I never understood it. Occasionally, he raised his hands or said something like he was in deep conversation with the air.

I placed my hand on Delores's shoulder and gave her a light shake. Startled, Delores jumped back. "Sorry," she said as she placed her hand over her heart. "You scared the salt out of me. It's a quarter to seven; why are you up so early?"

"Can't sleep. How could you not notice?" I pointed at the teakettle.

"Oh, that." Delores stood up and sliced a lemon. She squeezed it into a mug, and then poured in a stream of whiskey, boiling water, and a scoop of sugar. "We don't have honey," she said. She finally looked at me. "I don't know."

"What's going on?"

"I felt so alone last night." Delores stirred her drink around so many times the liquid formed a funnel. "I couldn't stop thinking about Gabriel. I doubt we'll try again. Look how things are now between me and you."

My stomach churned. "Don't do this to me," I told her, sealing the door of our conversation. She was trying to pull information from me. She was staging her thoughts so she could try to get me to relate with her. "I'm not falling for this!"

"What are you talking about?"

"I know what you're trying to do. I can't talk to you."

"What? I don't understand what you're saying." Delores pulled the spoon out of her cup and stared at me. I avoided her gaze so she couldn't see inside my thoughts. I looked at the mug instead. The hot drink whirled around. I felt dizzy all over.

"What's going on with you?"

"Nothing. I don't want to talk." I scrunched my hands into fists and dug my fingernails into my palms. She reached her hand out for one of my fists, but I pulled it back.

"You're trying to trap me into getting caught up in your conversations."

"Honestly, Manz, you're not making any sense."

"Whatever." I went into the bathroom and twisted the knobs of the shower. Hopefully, the sound of the streaming water would prevent her from reading my thoughts. After undressing, I stepped into the shower and leaned against the wall. I wished the water could somehow beat me down the drain so I could just disappear.

Why would Delores try to do something like that to me? I brought my hands to my face to wipe the water from my eyes. Red blotches popped through the skin on my arms. I cried out and tried wiping them off. The humming started again and I thrashed around trying to get rid of the infestations. I pinched one of the spots, but nothing came out, so I squeezed it harder.

I was about to cry out again, but I didn't want to alarm Delores. I gouged at my skin and dug until blood surfaced. I stared as the other blotches disappeared and the blood oozed from my arm and mixed with the water of the shower like paint rinsed from a brush. I watched the color wash down the drain, then sat down and leaned back against the wall.

I stared crying, my tears mixed with the water and the blood. Only part of me disappeared down the drain. Nothing made sense. Nothing.

You better be careful.

I looked around wildly to find the voice. I took several

deep breaths and hummed louder than the buzzing in my ears. My teeth chattered.

I stepped out of the shower and watched as gallons of water seemed to fall from my body. After I dressed in my room, Delores knocked on the door and then entered. "Did you have a chance to calm down? Manz, what happened to your arm?" Delores grabbed for a tissue and brought it close to me, but I squirmed away from her.

"I scratched a mosquito bite off."

Delores didn't look convinced. I knew she could tell I was lying. I bet she knew I was planning to leave. *I better get away from here soon*, I thought.

"You need to see a doctor," Delores said, confirming that she was out to trap me.

"It's just a little blood. There's nothing wrong with me." I tried to speak slowly so the panic wouldn't leak out. "What time should I drop you off at work?"

"I don't think you should drive."

"What'll convince you that I'm fine?"

"I'll call Joanne." Her face was pale. She looked like she did after she came home from her mother's funeral.

I told myself I was in control. "Please don't."

THE RIDE TO THE Mart was so silent I covered my left ear to thwart the humming and to make sure that none of the noise in my head spilled out.

When Delores looked at me, her eyes said that there weren't enough circus peanuts in the world to fix me. "You better be safe," she said as she stepped out of the car. "You and Jed do something fun today." Delores slipped a ten-dollar bill into my hand.

"Thanks." I rolled the money between my fingers and slipped it in my pocket before driving off to pick up Jed. While waiting, I honked the horn loudly and massaged the tension in my neck.

Sally walked out of the house like a ghost. I unbuckled the seat belt and rolled down the window. "You okay?"

"Sure, but listen, I just came out to tell you that Jed might be a few more minutes. Dad got mad at Jed. Jed doesn't know when to shut up."

"And he gets mad at you when you do. Are you keeping some kind of secret that'll get you in more trouble than it's worth?"

She barely smiled. Her features seemed so fragile. Thin lips. Little nose. Small eyes. "It's not like that really. It's about this place," Sally said and looked out toward the orchard. "Some things don't last forever."

Sally glanced to the left and then to the right. "If my dad sees me talking to you out here, I'll be the next to get in trouble."

"I understand," I said as she started walking away. Even though my nerves were on high alert, I felt calmed after seeing Sally.

I leaned back in the driver's seat and tried to relax while I waited for Jed. He came out in a few minutes, his cheek reddened and puffy.

"Sally told me what happened." I expected Jed to stink from nerves, but he didn't.

"He really *can* go to hell," Jed said. "I hope someone sends him there soon."

WHEN JED AND I crossed the tracks of the Great Divide, we saw two guys standing at the corner waiting for jobs. Baseball caps covered their dark faces, but from what I could see, they looked a few years older than Jed and me.

"This spot is taken," one of the guys said when we got close enough. "You white boys go home and ask your daddies for money."

"Go back to Mexico!" Jed yelled back at them. "I bet the Border Patrol is on its way."

Both of the guys lunged at Jed.

"Hey!" I threw Jed back and stood in front of him. "We got a job; we're not going to take yours."

"You and your friend better get away from here," the other guy said. I pushed Jed down the street to prevent any fighting. Jed finally had the sense to shut up.

We stood almost a block away, but I saw their triangular eyes daring us to get closer. Minutes ticked by, but I couldn't stop staring in their direction.

Smithson Darby pulled around the corner and slowed in front of the two guys waiting to get work, but drove down the road to pick us up. "You boys playing games?" he asked. Without wanting to, I looked in the direction of those guys again. "You got to stand your ground against those burros," Smithson Darby said. Jed snickered.

In the back of the truck, my head whirled from anger and confusion. "I should've let you get whomped for the second time today."

"What are you talking about?"

"You want to send me back to Mexico?" I could taste copper in the back of my throat.

"You ain't an illegal."

"How do you know if those guys were from Mexico anyway? What about my father?"

"It's just talk, Manz."

"We can talk too." I held my fist close to his already puffy face.

His face turned so red I could barely see his freckles. I backed off. When we arrived at the ranch, Jed chopped up a post until it shattered into mesquite toothpicks.

"Feel better?" I called over to him.

"Not yet!" Jed took a final swing at the remaining splinters of the post.

"I didn't mean to get so upset," I finally said. He didn't respond, but it should've been him saying sorry to me. Jed never used to be so angry—well, at least so angry at everything.

When the lunch bell rang, Jed refused to come with me; he still refused to say anything. When I walked into the dining hall, Vanessa's face showed instant relief. It seemed like I was in line forever before I finally had a chance to speak with her.

"Hey you," she said as she slid me a glass of tea.

"I wanted to call you last night," I said, finally feeling brave. "But . . . " I wasn't smart enough to come up with an excuse. When I was with her, I felt like holding back.

"I'm glad you thought of it," Vanessa said with a smile that accentuated her wide-set eyes. "Where's Stinky?"

"Still working." I had the feeling, though, that Jed was talking about me, stirring up some kind of trouble.

Before I slid my tray down the line, Vanessa said, "We're having a family barbeque this weekend. You're welcome to come if you'd like." She said it so casually I was disappointed.

"You're going to barbeque your family?" I tried to joke, but it came out sounding idiotic. It's something Jed or Tom would say, but I couldn't pull it off. Vanessa stared at me blankly.

"Sorry," I said, trying to cover my stupidity. "I'd be honored to meet your family."

"Not eat them." Vanessa filled up several glasses with ice. "I'll call you sometime this week to give you directions." Then she whispered, "Your cheeks are as red as *manzanas*."

I stared at the brown tray in my hands to see if there were any initials, but it just had some light scratches. I felt like running out of there, but before I left, I picked out a sandwich for Jed.

PARASITE

The truck squealed down the street. I waited with an ill feeling for the jingling of keys, for Tom to walk through the front door with his gruff "Howdy." I didn't look out the window, in case any shadowy figures lurked there.

"Shouldn't you check to see if Tom is here?" I asked Delores, who'd been cooped up in the bathroom for an hour at least. I had the growing suspicion that it wasn't Tom outside and I was too afraid to look.

"In a minute," she said.

Who knew who could be out there?

Finally, the keys jingled and I heard the turning of the knob. "Aloha," Tom called out, thwarting my "Howdy" expectation.

"Aloha," I said back. "Have a good trip?"

"You're never going to believe this, but a chicken jumped up into my grille when I was driving back into town."

My mind flashed to the boy chasing after the chicken outside the Mart. Delores probably mentioned what happened and maybe this was Tom's way of trying to make a joke of it.

"You look kind of serious there, Manzoil. Did I ever tell you this one?" Tom asked. I knew he was trying to get me sidetracked.

"So a grizzled old man was eating in a truck stop when three Hells Angels bikers walked in. The first walked up to the old guy, pushed his cigarette into the old man's mashed potatoes and then took a seat at the counter. The second Hells Angel spit in the old man's milk and then took a seat at the counter. The third walked up to the old man, turned over the old man's plate, and then took a seat at the counter." Tom laughed the laugh that means the punch line is near.

"Well, without saying a damn thing, the old man left the diner. Right after, one of the bikers said to the waitress, 'What a sorry excuse for a man.' The waitress replied, 'Not much of a truck driver either; he just backed his big rig over three motorcycles.'" Tom cackled with laughter. "You like that one?"

"Haven't heard it before."

"Don't you think it's even the slightest bit funny? You must be holding your laughs in. That don't do you good, you know? Delores here?"

"Yeah, I'm here," Delores said, her voice muffled through the door. I didn't hear her laughing in the bathroom.

"You're just in time," she said. The bathroom door creaked open and Delores walked out. She was now a redhead with a streak of pumpkin orange in her bangs.

I stared at her. "You like it?" she asked Tom, and gave him a hug. She didn't look in my direction. I was glad not to have to answer the same question.

"You're my gal," Tom said with his hearty chuckle. I'm not sure what he found so funny all the time. "Maybe now I can lay off a few of those blonde jokes. Haven't heard too many good redhead ones."

"I missed you," Delores said. She leaned over and whispered something in his ear. I stood there feeling awkward until I realized she was probably telling him something about me.

"I can hear you," I said quietly, even though I couldn't make out what they were saying. But they kept whispering their whispers. "I hear you!"

They both stopped whispering and stared at me. "Have the guts to say it to my face!" I yelled.

Delores took her index finger and scratched her reddened scalp while Tom started laughing. "Don't think you'd want to hear what we're saying." He turned to Delores and said, "Big Tom has been lonely."

"You can't play it off." I felt frenzied—they were playing me. They were keeping tabs on me, trying to get to me, trying to find out my plans.

"Quit acting *loco*," Delores said as she walked over to me with a smile. Not a pretty young smile, but a devious smile, a smile that said she had some plans of her own. Delores placed her hands on my shoulders. She was forcing me to stay, forcing herself into my thoughts.

I pushed her off and marched out the front door.

"Manz?" I heard Delores call out as I walked down the driveway. A voice echoed through the window screens. *MANZ . . . Manz . . . manz . . .*

I wasn't sure where I was going at first. I knew not to get into the Nova and drive. Didn't want to give them a reason to take it away from me. I still heard Delores calling my name even though I was close to crossing the tracks of the Great Divide. I kept looking over my shoulder to see if they were following me.

I imagined Tom saying something like, "Just let the boy go, he'll come back somewhere." It wasn't his saying, exactly, but everything was too loud for me to think right. It sounded like there were people talking down the street, only I couldn't see anyone; I just heard their murmuring voices.

Tonight should be the night, I thought. I'd been ready for so long. I should've been out of here long ago. I should've been buying the ticket for the next train traveling away from Rockhill. *I should be . . . I should be . . .* a voice looped over and over again, until it was as confusing as the mumbling.

Not yet, I decided through the noise. I wasn't ready yet. I should've been, I knew. I'd felt ready for so long. But it wasn't the night. Why couldn't I be ready?

I continued walking to clear things in my mind. I kept my head focused straight ahead in case any scuttling shadows lurked around. I needed the night air. I felt like a parasite feeding from the tree's branches until I was ripe enough to leave. I realized I had to put up a border between me and the people I knew. I didn't want them to know where I was going. They'd prevent me from leaving.

I REMEMBER ONE NIGHT, after Jed's folks were asleep, Jed, Sally, and I walked through the orchard while the moonlight cast a soft blue spell.

"See that?" Sally asked, and of course Jed and I didn't know what we were trying to see. "It looks like mistletoe hanging from the tree."

"Maybe we should cut it off and hang it in Mama and Dad's doorway," Jed said.

I expected him to make a joke out of the mistletoe or tease Sally. Sally and I didn't respond, but we studied the rows and rows of apple trees, probably both thinking of the horrendous fight in the house earlier. Thankfully, no one had been hurt.

Still thinking of that night, I continued walking. The sound of the crunching voices lessened as I thought about Sally.

"The mistletoe is a parasite and if it stays like that, the branches will bulge because it holds back the flow of life. Ancient farmers put mistletoe on their trees," Sally had said.

"Why?" I asked her, staring at her in the pale moonlight. Jed didn't act interested. He never was, not when it came to the orchard.

"If farmers keep the growth down, the trees can grow

more apples." There was a long silence between the three of us and then Sally spoke again. "Druids used to say that apples grown on trees with mistletoe had special powers."

I stared at her longer, wondering how she knew this and how she would react if I tried kissing her under the mistletoe. It was too hokey though, and I couldn't. Not with Jed there.

MY LEGS ACHED, BUT I continued walking. There weren't as many trees on this side of the railroad tracks. There wasn't as much of anything because water was more restricted. Not across the Great Divide, not where water was sanctioned for the orchards.

A speckled black and white dog barked territorial war cries at me as I passed by. I continued walking on and listened to the threats of the dog's barking mixed with the mumbling noises.

I thought about Sally and her Druids to get the voices to hush up, but when I came upon the cemetery, I pushed her out of my thoughts. I didn't want to associate Sally with a cemetery.

LOS MUERTOS

The mumbling filled my head as I looked around the cemetery. The headstones were grouped closely together and I couldn't stop thinking about how many bodies were buried beneath the ground. *Los Muertos*. The Dead.

As far as I could see, the graveyard was empty, but I continued searching for the source of the noise.

I wasn't sure if the cemetery was my intended destination, but I was here now, so I sat on a bench. I noticed then how badly my feet throbbed. Silk flowers decorated most of the graves, some arranged in circles and some in the shape of crosses. For a moment, I smelled a hint of the mountain laurel again, but it faded before I had a chance to breathe the odor deep into my lungs.

Rockhill had two cemeteries, just like it had two gas stations, separated just the same. After Loco died, Delores tried to get enough money to bury him. There wasn't much money when he was alive, but now we couldn't afford a casket and a plot in the ground. Delores wrote a letter to her mother asking for money. I watched as she placed a stamp on it and I assumed she'd mailed it until I found the letter filed away.

Loco was cremated, just like Gabriel.

"Will it hurt?" I asked her.

"He's dead. Don't you understand?"

Of course I didn't. Tears formed in her eyes and I felt awful for talking about it, but there were so many things I needed to know.

"What're we going to do now?" I asked when she calmed down. Delores shrugged, then extended her arms and wrapped them around me.

Delores and I had a difficult time talking about Loco's death. Even years after he died, Delores would just sip her drink and change the subject. The closest we got was one night when Delores had drunk too much and told me, "Daddy was right. Your father was nothing but trouble."

"What do you mean?"

"Nothing," she said. "Absolutely nothing." She threw her glass against the wall. Glass shards sprayed everywhere. I cleaned them up after she stormed off.

My father and Delores had a big fight before he left. She was trying to convince him to go see a specialist, even though we didn't have the money.

"I'm fine!" he yelled at her.

Loco was driving on Highway 90 when he ran into a

guardrail. There were no witnesses and it took the authorities over three hours to find his body. They found alcohol in his system, but he wasn't over the legal limit, so the crash was ruled accidental.

Exactly how it happened is a mystery. But I had my suspicions, most likely from a memory that haunted me, a memory that grew more vivid as I got older.

Delores was gone one afternoon when I came home from school early. I walked through the door and Loco sat on the black leather couch, white like bleached sheets. The .22 caliber pistol was shoved so deep into his mouth that I couldn't see the barrel. His hand shook so much that the black handgun twitched. His lips were tightly pressed around the gun—they were white with a red ring around them. Like a target.

"Don't!" I yelled.

His eyes tracked me as I begged him not to shoot, the coffee table separating us. He cocked the hammer by pulling back the slide.

"Get that out of your mouth!" I approached him and he didn't flinch, so I got closer. He still didn't move, so I slowly made my way next to him on the couch. Then I squeezed him so hard my shoulders felt as though they'd slide out of their sockets. I clenched my teeth together in case the gun sounded.

Loco drew the gun out of his mouth and placed it in his lap. The gun faced me. Tears streamed down my father's face. I'd never seen him cry before. I grabbed the gun off of his lap and set it on the coffee table. Loco cried so deeply his body heaved.

THE MEMORY MADE ME feel shaky and afraid, but what freaked me out even more was that I couldn't be certain it happened. We never owned a black leather couch, yet I specifically recall the leather couch in my memory. My father never traveled with a gun, and the sheriff never found anything in the car either, just the lunch Delores packed for him.

I stared at the chiseled headstones. My father could've been buried there. Gabriel would've been buried on the other side of town.

Delores and I took my father's ashes to Jed Sr.'s orchard. We never told anyone about it, but we walked out there one morning, hours before the sun rose in the sky.

"He loved the trees best of all," she said after our prayer.

I wondered then if he loved me, but I knew he did. I let Delores spread the ashes because I was too afraid to see his remains.

"We have to hurry," Delores said, looking at Jed's house. I wasn't sure what would happen if we got caught.

Loco would've had silk flowers near his plot. Delores would've seen to that. But maybe he helped mistletoe grow on one of the apple trees instead.

I thought of the marble box in Gabriel's room. She didn't place silk flowers near it, but instead, a teddy bear with a blue silk ribbon tied around its neck.

"What are you going to do with it?" I asked Delores after she brought the box home. She looked at the teddy bear, even though she knew I meant Gabriel's ashes.

"I'm not sure," she said. I wondered if she was thinking about the night in the orchard too.

THE TEMPERATURE DROPPED SLIGHTLY during the time I sat there, reliving memories. Maybe that's the real reason I was directed to the cemetery. I watched the hairs on my arm stand on end and I swatted a mosquito. I felt weak and ready to go back to being a parasite. I didn't want to go back to the house, but I couldn't be at the cemetery any longer.

My knees buckled when I stood up from the bench and I shivered as I started walking back. My arm itched and when I looked at it, I saw the red dot left by the mosquito bite, but then it looked as if red blotches were forming again. I scratched my arm, trying to gouge out layers of skin. I ran back the same route I'd taken earlier.

I TRIED TO CATCH my breath and opened the door slowly, so I wouldn't make a scene. I felt like collapsing. Tom sat on the couch reading the newspaper. "I knew you'd come back," he said.

"How could you be so sure?" I asked between wheezes.

"Just knew," he said, probably sensing my weakness. "Your mother is worried about you."

"Where is she?"

"Asleep now."

"Bet she was so worried she drank herself to sleep. So, are you in on all of this too?" I wasn't sure if the words came out of my mouth.

"What are you on? Reefer? Acid? Meth?" Tom rubbed at his beard to fill the silence between us. Finally, he said, "Must be something good." He started to laugh his annoying laugh, which he didn't believe in holding in.

"I wish I knew," I answered, but I could feel myself starting to get sick. What if he made a joke because he and Delores slipped me something I didn't know about? I needed to be careful.

"You got me worried about you too." Before he got too serious, he asked, "You know why they call me the Ripper, don't you?"

The Ripper was Tom's truck-driving nickname. I shrugged my shoulders and started thinking of ways to get out of the conversation. Tom got up from the couch and poured some water into a coffee mug; he must've known how thirsty I was. He handed it to me, and despite my painful thirst, I let the mug slip through my fingers, staging an accident. Tom could've poisoned it.

He bent down to pick up the unharmed mug and walked over to the sink to refill it for me. I grabbed the container from him. "Don't worry about it. Not thirsty."

"Fine," Tom said and walked back to the couch, crunching the edge of the newspaper up when he sat down. "This one night, I was stoned with my buddies. A friend of mine, RJ, brought out a glass jar. When I bent over to look in the glass, there was a baby rattler inside." Tom laughed and looked over at me suspiciously, trying to figure me out, I'm sure. He didn't stand a chance, not even with poison.

"So I started laughing and tapped my finger on the glass, but when I did, that damn rattlesnake struck it. I was so shocked, I just let one rip right out. Rrrrrrip! Those boys never let me live that one down. Rrrrrrip!" Tom repeated and lifted his rear end off the couch to exaggerate. The newspaper crinkled.

"Don't think that's funny either, huh?" Tom asked. "Guess it was one you just had to be there for."

"I guess." I smiled, but I couldn't bring myself to laugh. Tom did that enough for the both of us. I walked to my room, hoping it wouldn't be my room for much longer.

Tom yelled down the hall, "I'm here if you want to talk."

"You wouldn't understand."

DEAD POLES

I continued to twist the key in the starter, but the engine just rumbled a bronchial cough and refused to turn over.

"Pop the hood, Manz," Tom said.

I hesitated for a moment, thinking Tom might've been putting something in the engine to make the Nova fall apart. But then I started thinking of how Vanessa was waiting for me to show up at the barbeque, and I decided I didn't care. When I'd told her I was coming, she clapped her hands together and said she was excited. All that day, I kept thinking about her smile.

I got out of the car and watched as Tom twisted wires and clanked around in the guts of the car. He knew what he was doing, but I watched him carefully to see if he loosened any cap that shouldn't be loosened or cut any wires that shouldn't be cut.

"Try it now," he said. When it came to vehicles, Tom was all business.

I got in the front seat and when I turned the key, I half expected some sort of explosion. That wouldn't have made sense though, not with Tom standing right there. He wouldn't have wanted the accident to involve himself, would he? Delores needed him, even if Gabe was gone. I turned the key again, but still, the Nova didn't start.

"The car is too old," I told Tom.

"Nonsense," he said, "she's just taking a breather." He grabbed more tools and fished around in the engine for a cure.

Looking at Tom, the nickname the Ripper seemed appropriate. If you didn't know the whole story, a name like the Ripper sounded like a murderer's nickname. Tom could've passed for a serial killer.

With beads of sweat on his forehead, Tom pulled himself out from under the hood of the car. "I think I need more time to tinker with the engine. I'll give you a lift wherever you need to go, as long as you don't mind riding in the rig."

Maybe he'd staged the car trouble to monitor me. I was quiet as I thought of Vanessa's face again. Her directions were secured in my pocket.

"Fine." I figured he could let me off down the street, so her family wouldn't see him.

Tom wiped his greasy, blackened hands on a towel and then scratched his chin. A black line of filth smeared on his face. It almost looked like blood.

"So, you like this girl?" Tom asked when we got into his truck and headed toward Herman.

"Maybe. Big damn deal."

Tom started asking questions and talking just like Delores. He was trying to invite himself into a place he wasn't wanted. He'd just try to make a blueprint of my thoughts and my weaknesses, and if he found out Vanessa was one of these weaknesses, he'd use it against me.

I thought about telling Vanessa I wasn't interested in her, or that I had a girlfriend. I thought of all the lies I could tell to push her away, and felt certain they would've worked too. Why had I involved her? I should've been simplifying things, not complicating them.

But Vanessa intrigued me. I told her I would come and I couldn't lie to her.

"So did you come up with any redhead jokes?" I asked Tom, desperate to change the subject.

"I did, but you ain't going to find them funny." He sounded hurt. Maybe he knew I was thinking about him being a murderer. Maybe he knew I was worried about what stunts he might've pulled.

"Try me," I said, attempting to sound convincing. I knew I had to start putting on an act with everyone. I couldn't let them read my mind like that. I had to think of ways to prevent it.

"So, I was thinking of this joke," Tom said, "but I don't think it's one I'd tell Delores." He looked over at me like he was trying to feign confidentiality. "So how do you know if a redhead's in love with you?

"If she follows you everywhere your truck goes, pitches a tent outside of it, and puts your new girlfriend in the hospital, you know she's yours."

I laughed about the same time he started laughing, but the laughter didn't sound real. I wasn't even sure what my real laugh sounded like anymore. Tom looked pleased though.

"Here's another one I wouldn't tell Delores. How do you get a redhead to argue with you?" Tom asked, waiting for me to answer.

I shrugged my shoulders.

"You say something."

Nervous, I started laughing, but I was getting sucked up into Tom's confidence. *I need to be more careful*, I told myself. Not play all those games with everyone.

I felt myself calming down and I gave Tom the directions he needed to get to Herman. "Turn left," I said after we passed Main Street. She lived across the tracks, not on the border like me.

We passed by a Catholic church with its rocks crumbling and the sign tilting.

I saw what looked like a totem pole at the end of a street. "Stop here." I started worrying that Tom's truck might be too noisy. Maybe Vanessa could hear us driving over and regretted inviting me.

"Here? There's nothing around."

"I know where I'm at." I remembered how Vanessa said when you see the wooden pole, her house was up the drive. "Please, if you could just drop me off."

"If that's what you want," Tom said. "What time should I pick you up?"

"I'll call when I'm ready." I slammed the door to his rig. Vanessa was right when she said how far her house was from everything.

I heard laughter drifting through the air and I looked around me to see if anyone had followed me. When I got closer to the house, smoke floated from a barbeque pit. A group of people both stood and sat around. I was relieved to see the noise coming from them.

Vanessa rushed toward me. "Isaiah, you made it!" Heads turned and stared at me. I turned away from their eyes, which looked triangular and menacing. I slowed down the pace of my steps. I stood and inspected another one of the totem poles. When I looked around, I noticed several more lining the drive and about three posted in front of the house.

On the top of the pole was a skeleton face, painted white with features outlined in black. Other animals and shapes were carved below it.

"So what do you think?" a voice asked, sneaking up behind me. It took me a moment to realize it was Vanessa's.

"I've never seen anything quite like it."

"That's what everyone says. I sort of combined Native American traditions with Mexican folk art styles."

"You made these?" I asked her, feeling stupid in front of Vanessa and her family. I knew they were out there on the porch watching my reaction, listening to all of my thoughts and words.

"My grandfather taught me to carve when I was younger. When they started clearing the land years ago, I used the mountain cedar to carve what I call *Los Postes de Muertos*. I made them to honor our relatives for *Día de los Muertos*."

Dead Posts. I stared at her in amazement. I closed my eyes for a moment to think of how sinuous her arms must've looked while she was carving. I tried not to think of the sadness in Delores's eyes when she first started painting. "They're amazing."

Vanessa leaned over and kissed me on my cheek. I immediately looked toward the barbecue pit.

"How'd you make them?" I asked, trying my best to stall.

"I used the trees with the most imperfections—the ones with character. I smoothed away the bark and drew pictures on the wood and let the figures sort of come out to me when I started carving. After, I painted the poles. Simple, really."

"Simple? Sure. How long does it take?" I thought of a million other questions to ask so I wouldn't have to face her family.

"The small poles take about a month or two, and bigger ones, like this one," Vanessa said and patted the Dead Post, "can take over six months. I sometimes work on several poles at once. I started selling a few to save up for school."

I stared at the pole a moment longer. I wanted her to carve something for me after I was gone.

OPERATION WETBACK

Vanessa's father cleared his throat loudly before shaking my hand. "A pleasure, Isaiah."

"And you too, Mr. Ortiz." The look on his face said that meeting me wasn't so pleasurable. I met Vanessa's younger sister, Wilnelia, as well as several cousins, aunts, and uncles. They all smiled at me and welcomed me, but I didn't feel welcomed. I was the only non-family member, other than Wilnelia's giggly friend.

"Is your grandfather here?" I whispered to Vanessa. I wanted to meet the man who taught Vanessa magic.

"He died years ago," she said. "I made my first pole for him."

"I'm sorry," I told her, realizing we had both lost important people. I stood away from the group and watched the family's eyes light up talking to each other. They didn't look so menacing, but a few aunts and uncles were sanctioned off and I couldn't help but wonder if they were talking about me. My suspicions were confirmed when they glanced in my direction.

Vanessa kind of scooted me to the side. "You can relax, Manz."

The tickle of her hot breath against my neck lingered. I felt relief hearing my name. Vanessa hadn't called me Manz once since I'd arrived.

"We don't barbeque each other and we aren't going to grill you."

I laughed for her, just as I laughed for Tom. I didn't want to tell her I couldn't relax when so many people were talking about me.

Finally, in his deep-throated voice, Vanessa's father broadcasted, "Dinner is ready!" Upon the announcement, her family gathered in a circle around the pit and said a prayer.

I wondered if, had things worked out differently between Loco and Delores, we would've had huge family gatherings. I'd always wanted to meet Loco's parents and family, although I was less interested in Delores's.

We ate chicken fajitas outside. "These are delicious," I said, and her family seemed pleased.

"Where do you go to school?" several people asked. "Got any brothers or sisters?" I answered quickly and helped myself to seconds to avoid talking.

Plates removed, we sat outside and watched as the day officially turned into night. The lighting was minimal and when I turned, I saw too many shadows and heard whispering. I decided to hold my head as still as possible to focus on the glowing coals in the barbeque pit. I knew I'd cause too much suspicion otherwise.

Finally, some of the aunts and uncles said they had better get going because of the long drive. They kissed Vanessa and her parents on the cheek and said goodnight.

"Should I call Tom to pick me up?" I asked Vanessa, not sure if I should stay or go.

Like he was reading my mind, Mr. Ortiz leaned over and said, "You're welcome to stay."

"Thank you, sir," I answered, trying to keep the nerves out of my voice. I was ready to leave or have some alone time with Vanessa.

Most of her family left, but I couldn't ignore the whispering. *Listen*, a voice said above the noise. It sounded like my father's voice, just like when I heard it before. I looked around to see who might've said it. No one paid attention, not even Vanessa. *Listen*.

I tried coaching myself not to panic and kept my head still as could be. The coals burned red hot. *Listen*.

"I am," I said to the voice. Vanessa turned to look at me, but I played it off. I listened to the whispering to understand what I was supposed to be hearing. The fajitas soured in my stomach. I wanted to call Tom so I could leave.

Listen, the voice repeated. I felt like screaming, "I'm listening! I'm listening!"

We moved inside the house and I worried I might get sick. Wilnelia and her friend went into a room and I wished Vanessa and I could've broken away too. I kept waiting for the voice to say something again. I gouged at my fingernails, just waiting.

Vanessa's mom brought out another plate of Mexican wedding cookies. I selected one of the powder-dusted crescents out of respect for her, even though my stomach rolled. I worried that the cookie might've contained something to make me confess. I had no intentions of hurting them. I just liked their daughter.

"Where are you from?" Vanessa's mom asked.

I swallowed hard. "The Valley, Pecos, Rockhill . . . it seems like all over sometimes." I leaned over and helped myself to another cookie even though it was the last thing I wanted.

"You Mexican?" her father asked. I felt like spitting the cookie across the room. How could he ask me something like that? He was a man who'd obviously raised a family with some type of Mexican bloodline. Maybe he sensed I was part white.

LISTEN! the voice yelled so loud my inner ear canal vibrated. I couldn't help it, but stared at all their faces looking at me. The voice wasn't one of theirs, but I didn't know where it was coming from. Vanessa and her parents didn't seem afraid. How could they not have been afraid with someone yelling so loudly? Tears welled up in my eyes.

"You don't have to be ashamed," her father said, confusing me even more. I had to control myself. They could see through me. "Are you legal?" he asked.

"Yes, sir. My father grew up in Mexico, but I've never been there. Someday I'll go." I felt stronger saying it. *Maybe I'll go to Mexico when I leave Rockhill*, I thought. *Maybe I could eventually find my father's relatives.*

"We taught Vanessa to be proud of her heritage," he said. I looked over at him. In her father's glassy eyes, I saw the reflection of the ceiling fan spinning around and around. I thought of grabbing another Mexican wedding cookie to act calmer, but I couldn't bring myself to eat anything more.

"My father came to the United States, just a boy still, after the Second World War," Mr. Ortiz continued. "A slick coyote promised my father a contract when he came to Texas. Here, he met Vanessa's grandmother, the daughter of a bracero who was promised things too. Both were illegals."

Mr. Ortiz cleared his gravelly throat and waited for a moment to continue. I looked down at my shoes to avoid the spinning fans in his eyes. "They had three children and I was the oldest. My parents were illegals, but not us. We were citizens, born in the United States. We didn't know the freedoms we were promised and Texas didn't care." He paused again, just like Tom did when he told a joke, only he was serious.

I looked back at him and stared again at his eyes and the reflection of the spinning ceiling fan. There was something almost godlike about him when he spoke.

"The government passed Operation Wetback to get rid of the illegals. We were dropping prices, becoming too expendable. Border Patrol, the military, police—everyone kidnapped the illegals and sent them back to Mexico.

"My father and our family were repatriated to Durango, Mexico. The authorities didn't care if we died. As long as we never came back. My parents never did, but I was determined to return. I was a citizen."

I looked at him a moment, my mind buzzing with questions about Operation Wetback.

Mr. Ortiz's eyes met mine. "You won't find this in your school textbook," he said. Again, it felt like he'd read my mind.

"My Vanessa and Wilnelia will also grow up fighting injustices, by being successful." He gave me a look, almost warning me not to try to prevent them.

But I didn't need the warning; I knew nothing could hold Vanessa back.

"And you will be too," he said, clapping his big hand against my back.

I wondered how he could be certain. Who knew if success for me would ever be possible?

THE MESSENGER

A burst of laughter from Wilnelia and her friend shattered the intensity in the living room. The four of us sat stiffly, with the past displayed before us like a patient on an operating room table.

I felt too numb to ask any questions about Operation Wetback. So I listened as Mr. Ortiz said, "I guarantee you there will be another phase of Operation Wetback. Look at the many raids taking place all over the country."

I listened.

I listened. My pulse pounded. I listened. That's what the voice had told me to do.

The previous times I had heard the voice was when Jed threatened Sally and when I went to the cemetery. The voice was warning me, I suddenly realized. The thoughts made sweat gush from my pores and the room whirled. The voice was a messenger.

Maybe my father was trying to tell me something, leading me to some sort of an answer. *There was a reason I came here*, I realized. A reason I hadn't left Rockhill yet. I had to be ready for the message.

"Isaiah?"

"What?" I wasn't sure who called out my name.

"Mom mentioned it was getting late," Vanessa said.

"Sorry." My face burned with embarrassment. "I never knew any of this."

"Don't worry, Isaiah. I don't want your parents getting worried. We would be happy to give you a ride home," Mrs. Ortiz said.

"Thank you, but I told my father I'd call when it was time." I felt shaky as soon as I said it out loud. Tom wasn't my father. Could Loco hear what I said? *Don't be angry*, I begged.

"Do you need a drink of water?" Mrs. Ortiz asked.

Control your emotions! I screamed inside of myself. *Control them!*

"No. I just need some fresh air. May I use your phone?" I asked Vanessa's mother.

"Sure," she said, and led me to their den. When I picked up the phone to call Tom, I wondered if it was the same phone Vanessa used to call me. It might've been tapped. *Focus!* I screamed inside at myself. *Focus!* I looked around to see if anyone heard the racket. They left me alone.

On the fourth ring, Tom picked up the phone. "Hola," he said in a sarcastic tone.

I asked him to pick me up and whispered for him to hurry just as he hung up. I felt as if I would explode if I didn't get outside soon. When I walked back into the living room, Vanessa and her parents stared at me. They must've talked about the voices when I was away. *You're too transparent!* I screamed at myself.

"He's on his way," I said through all the yelling inside my head. While we waited, we made small talk about working on the fence. After five minutes, I glanced at my watch. "I guess I should go outside to wait for my ride."

Mr. Ortiz stood up to shake my hand. I wanted to bolt. "You are welcome here anytime," Mr. Ortiz said, like I'd passed some exam.

I thanked them as Mrs. Ortiz gave me a plate of Mexican wedding cookies to take home to share with my family. I felt sick looking at them.

"I better be on my way." Vanessa looked over at her parents and they nodded, giving her permission to accompany me outside.

"I thought your father was dead," she said when we were outside.

"Shh," I said, warning her. "He is. I slipped and said father instead of stepfather. Your parents would've asked too many questions. I'm sorry."

"Well, I'm sorry if they were boring, Manz. My father doesn't know when to shut it," Vanessa said, looking back to make sure her parents couldn't hear. It felt good hearing her say my name again.

"He had some important things to say." I didn't tell her all the realizations I'd come to. I didn't want to scare her off. But that's what I'd have to do anyway. No *Quinceañeros*, no sweet tea, nothing else.

I traced my hand over the tallest of the Dead Posts. The ridges of the wood scratched my fingertips. It was too dark to study the color of the paint Vanessa used. "You know you are going to be successful, don't you?" I asked her.

She scrunched her eyebrows together. "I guess so. What are you talking about?"

"Well, you will be." I stared at the carvings she created. I stayed silent for a moment, reflecting on her strength and artistic talent. The silence seemed unending and the mumbling crept upon me.

"My father doesn't know when to quit talking about history," Vanessa finally said, removing herself from the proximity of Operation Wetback.

"Those were things I needed to know."

"When you were on the phone, my dad said he liked you. It's a pretty big deal when he likes someone. He said there was something strong and deep about your eyes. He believes that a person's eyes are a defining characteristic."

"Your eyes remind me of Egypt," I said. I didn't explain what I meant, but she smiled.

Tom's truck rumbled along eventually, and his headlights illuminated the driveway.

I quickly kissed Vanessa on the lips. She kissed me back.

Her lips were soft, not like her hands. I wanted to wrap my arms around her and hold her for a long while.

Tom was quiet when he picked me up. No "howdy," no "aloha," no "hola." Maybe he knew I had called him my father. Would he be ashamed to be my father?

I turned up the volume on the radio to hush all the mumbling, but the mumbling couldn't be hushed away. *Just tune it out*, I commanded myself. *Just tune it out and figure it out*, I started singing inside my head.

"Did something happen?" I asked Tom, when I was about to lose it from repeating the words. Tom kept scratching at his beard and didn't try to fill the silence with a joke.

"Nothing new," Tom said. "Got an assignment. This one's going to be a long haul and Delores doesn't want me to go."

"She drinks more when you're gone," I said. Tom didn't argue with me. "You took the job for sure?"

"You know how contracts go—low wages, blah blah blah, but this one ain't a bad job. If I didn't take this one, then I'll start getting bad jobs. It's like what those tree hugging folks are always saying, if you kill a garter snake, then a rattler will take its place."

"How can you ignore her drinking?" I asked. I couldn't stand holding everything in any longer.

"She's a good gal. She tries hard, I know that."

"I saw her drinking when she was pregnant."

"What happened was genetic."

Tom's tone was venomous, and I didn't have the courage

103

to say more. I tried to deal with the mumbling, the static coming from the CB, and the thoughts of Gabriel's death.

"I fixed the Nova up," Tom said when we finally pulled into the driveway. "That'll give you a little freedom."

Did he know? Was he trying to encourage me to leave? Was he angry with me?

"Thanks." I slammed the truck door after we pulled into the driveway. *Not much longer now*, I thought to myself.

Delores reeked of whiskey and anger when I walked inside. I smelled it all over the place. *Say it*, the Messenger commanded. *Say it.*

I hesitated for a moment, but I looked at her and trusted the Messenger. "It's your fault Gabriel is dead. You killed him!"

I left the room before Delores could react. I had to cut the ties. Maybe that's what the Messenger reasoned too. I plugged my fingers in my ears in case Delores started crying. My head felt like it was going to implode as I fell into bed.

EYES

"Do you have to take this job?" Delores asked as Tom was leaving.

"What do your birthday, our anniversary, and a toilet all have in common?" Tom asked, squeezing her hand.

Delores shrugged her shoulders.

"I always miss them." Tom let go of her hand. He laughed. Delores didn't. "I'll miss you."

"Take care of yourself, Manzoil," Tom said.

The engine of Tom's truck revved up and then the sounds of his truck disappeared. I hadn't cut the ties right between Tom and me. No, after watching the truck pull down the street, I knew I didn't cut them right at all. There were some things I wanted to thank him for.

I got dressed by throwing on my old jeans. They were turning more yellow, like me. White salt crystals created a ring around the collar and the armpits of my shirt. For a moment, I worried I was late picking Jed up for work, but it was Sunday.

When I walked into the kitchen for a glass of water, Delores shook out the last few drops of a liquor bottle and tossed it into the trash. It clinked as it hit another bottle.

I saw the stack of Tom's letters piled up on the table. Delores hadn't touched them. Her hair was pinned up in rollers and I started to laugh.

"What's so funny?" Delores didn't look at me; instead she searched around all the cabinets looking for other bottles she might've hidden and forgotten about.

"How do you get a redhead's mood to change?" I asked, mimicking Tom's voice. I felt my laughter building to a roar. "You wait five seconds or until she can't find her whiskey!"

"Is this some sad cry for attention?"

It's working, I told myself. Laugh. Laugh. Laugh. Cut. Cut. Cut.

I finally stopped laughing because I felt a buzzing in my head. Maybe it was the poison they'd slipped me. I ran over to the sink and spat out the water, but it was already flowing through my system and calming me down.

"I can't change what's happened. Lord, I wish I could change a lot of things."

"Like me?" I asked under my breath.

"Jesus help me. First your father and now you." She sighed and wiped away her tears. I couldn't say anything else.

"I'm scheduled to work today," she said.

"What time?" I gazed down at my watch to avoid looking at her.

"Drop me off whenever." She was still searching for something to take the edge off. I doubt she could find anything that would.

"So you can have time to walk to the liquor store?"

"What does it matter to you?"

"You have a problem."

"And right now, it's you!"

I stormed outside to wait until she was ready to go. When she walked out, she looked more like herself, but somehow empty.

In the car, I flipped the radio on to a loud rock station. Delores reached over to change the dial to a country channel, but there was no music. The announcer said that a new report showed that the border crackdown was working.

I immediately flipped the station back, increasing the volume so loud the dash vibrated. Delores didn't touch anything; she sat back in the seat with her arms crossed tightly across her chest.

My throat itched to say something, but I wasn't sure how to form the words. I shouldn't have been caring as much as I did right then. I thought about saying, "I don't hate you." Even with the radio on so loud, the muttering ate away at my ears.

When we got to the Mart, Jay Jackson's beady eyes stared me down. There was nothing but hate in those eyes.

"Don't work today," I said, some of my words forming.

Jay Jackson looked like the real murderer, not Tom. Maybe we could go to a park and guess what God was doing. Sit and have all the conversations we'd been avoiding. I felt so confused because of the voices. I couldn't make out what they were trying to say.

"I have to work."

"You should be painting," I said. "I want you to be happy."

Delores caught my eye before stepping out of the car. "Me too. That's what I want for you. I'll see you later."

I wanted to go for a long drive, but I decided to go over to Jed's. The buzz was still too intense, so I stayed in the parking lot a moment longer, waiting for it to quiet. I closed my eyes, thinking about how, for the longest time, Delores couldn't take me to the site where my father crashed. "I just can't," she'd said. I even thought about asking Tom, but I wanted it to be more private.

Delores barely drove before the accident, and after, her fears just grew. When Tom bought the Nova after I got my permit, that spot on Highway 90 was the first place I wanted to go. "I need to," I said. "I'll go alone if I have to."

Delores didn't say anything, just rode in the car with me. I'd never driven so cautiously in my life. She held onto the handrest so hard that I could see the white bones of her knuckles through her skin.

It was a long drive down Highway 90. I kept thinking I was going to see something significant.

I wanted to ask Delores if she thought the accident happened because of his drinking. Did she think he did it on purpose? Did he get distracted? She looked so sick I figured I'd better not ask.

"Turn off on the shoulder," Delores said, pointing at a spot off the road.

I still thought I was going to see something life-changing. Repaired, the guardrail gave no sign it had claimed my father's life. The only thing not mended was us. This was where my father died, and there was nothing important about the spot.

When I got out of the car to look at the location, I saw a faded silk flower wreath several feet away from the railing. I loved Delores so much right then that it hurt.

I sat in Jay Jackson's parking lot a moment longer, playing the memories in my mind like movies in a theater. I spied Jay Jackson peeking out of a window.

Get out of here or die! I heard him thinking.

"You die!" I sped out of the parking lot. I escaped from the Mart, but I had a sick feeling Delores might not still be alive when I came back.

When I reached Jed's place, Sally pried the blinds open. Everyone was watching me through windows. When I parked the Nova and got out of the car, the sun sparkled so brightly I had to squint to avoid the glare. Even in the day, I couldn't escape the shadows.

When I knocked on the door, sweat pooled under my arms. I'd been scared at Jed's before, but not quite this kind of nervous. What if Tom and Delores contacted them about me? What if Jed's family was in on something?

Thankfully, it was Jed's mom who opened the door and not the old man. "Jedediah is in his room."

"Thank you, Mrs. Parker."

I walked to Jed's room in the back of the house, not wanting to bring any more attention to myself. A metal guitar from Jed's CD player blared. Before I reached his room, a hand stretched toward me. I almost screamed.

"Hush." Sally placed her index finger over my lips. "You got to look out for Jed," she whispered.

"Why?"

She spoke so low, I had to strain to hear her above the mumbling and metal guitar. "Dad's been more angry and the whole place is falling apart. That's what the whole thing is about, you know—this place."

"Rockhill?"

"In its own way, but more the orchard and this house. Or the people in it. Jed is going to hear us, but listen, Manz, you have to get him under control. He keeps threatening to do things and he even pushed Mama after she put ice on his face." Sally's eyes looked even more desperate.

"I'll do what I can," I said, void of any promise. The way she glanced at me, I knew I couldn't cut all the ties I needed to. I couldn't say no to her either, because really, who else did she have? But I wasn't the one she needed. I couldn't do the fixing she asked for.

Sally squeezed my hand and went back into her world of books and ancient Druids. I knocked to enter Jed's world. No answer. I knocked again.

"Come in!" Jed bellowed.

I hesitated for a moment, wondering if I should leave. I hadn't promised Sally anything. Instead, I pushed past the heavy weight of his door. Jed lay on his bed with his face buried in a pillow. He didn't have to say anything about what happened. It was the same story, just told in a different way. Jed nodded his head. "What's up?"

"You want to get out of here?" I asked.

"For good?"

"At least for a little while." When I left Rockhill, I wanted to leave on my own. Our friendship had changed so much and I couldn't trust him like I used to. He had to find his own way out.

"Let's go for a drive," I said, not thinking of any better way to get Jed's mind off things.

"Fine."

Before I started the Nova, I saw myself from an out-of-body perspective driving down Highway 90. I didn't crash into a guardrail—I crashed into a Dead Post. I saw the skeleton on the top and the shapes and patterns of the figures carved below it. My body jumped forward. I closed my eyes, and when I reopened them, I was sitting back in the driver's seat, shaking violently.

GATORS

The blast of the wind through the car windows did nothing to drown out the mumbling. Jed massaged his cheekbones, trying to rub away the pressure building in his face. I realized his nose was probably broken when I saw the lump in the middle.

"Do you need to go to the hospital?" I worried a dislodged piece of bone might get sucked into his brain.

"No, he's the one that should be going. I should've put him there," Jed said, pulling his hands away from his face.

Things were too loud and I couldn't keep driving with the buzzing in my head. I was about to ask Jed if he felt the same sensation, but one look gave me the answer. He looked even more miserable. I pulled the Nova to the side of the road.

"Want to hike Fantasma Hill, like old times?" I asked Jed, trying to overcome the noise.

"Whatever."

When we exited the car, Jed looked around like he was worried his father had followed us. He must've heard the buzzing too.

I tied the laces of my boots tight, thinking of how we used to hike up these hills when we were young. We even tried camping there one night, but Jed told some murder stories about Ol' Joe Ball who killed women by feeding them to five hungry gators. We weren't even sure what noises alligators made, but up on that hill, we heard them loud and clear coming from Fantasma Creek. Jed and I ran back to his house, stopping frequently to catch our breath and rest our feet from the long trip back. The first person Jed checked on was his mother. I checked on Sally. Then I called Delores.

"WHY DON'T YOU CALL the sheriff?" I asked him.

"They've never done anything before. Mama won't press charges. She's too afraid of what he'll do. I thought about pressing them, but he'll make it sound like I'm the one at fault. Besides, he'll have it in for me later, or he'll take it out on Mama or Sally."

The swishing of voices around me was too much. It wasn't like the voice of the Messenger, just the whispering of voices crowded around me. Nothing they said was clear. I plugged my fingers in my ears and started humming.

Jed pulled my hands away from my head. "What are you doing?"

"You can't hear it?"

"I don't hear anything. What the hell are you talking about?"

Be quiet! I screamed inside myself. *Be quiet!*

"Nothing." I sucked in a deep breath and tried to gain control. "I have an earache." Jed shook his head and laughed at me.

We were quiet as we started hiking. My calf muscles burned from moving so fast. The buzzing didn't stop, but all around me, background noises popped out even louder—the honking of a horn and the aggravated fussing of a mockingbird.

Things around me seemed brighter too, just like the day at the ranch. A black and green iridescent beetle scuttled around on the red dirt. When I passed by a sotol plant, I stared at how the spiny edges of the leaves seemed sharper. Standing in the middle of a deep yellow green sotol stood a tall, dry stalk. Vanessa could've smoothed it down to create a walking stick.

Jed walked by the plant and, grabbing the stalk, he snapped it in half. I heard the fibrous strands ripping so loudly I winced.

"Why'd you do that? Vanessa can't make anything out of it now."

"What would Vanessa do with it anyway? You keep looking around like you're stressed out or something. You're freaking me out." Jed tossed the pieces to the ground. They thudded as they hit the earth.

"She's an artist. She carves things. You should see these poles she made—like totem poles."

"Did you get together with her or what?"

"I went to her place . . . "

"Did she touch your pole?" Jed laughed.

"No, it wasn't like that at all. But I kissed her. At the end. Mostly, I spent time with her family and things started to make sense. It was like a piece of the missing puzzle."

"If you ask me," Jed said, "you're still missing it."

When we reached the tallest part of Fantasma Hill over-looking Rockhill, Jed and I stared at all the minuscule houses and trees laid out in perfect rows. It was all geometry from up there. I surveyed the tracks running through town. If I struggled enough, I could've found Tom's house.

After a silent spell, Jed said, "He first started hitting Mama because dinner wasn't on time. He came in from the orchard at five-thirty sharp. Dinner should be on the table at five-thirty sharp. Well, it wasn't."

I continued staring at the lines and the squares of the town.

"He had her pinned in the corner. He punched her in the gut and she fell to the ground."

His father wouldn't dare hit his mother in her beautiful face—not where the marks showed the most. It never mattered where he hit Jed though.

"I grabbed a pot and swung it at him, but I missed. Then he started whaling on me. Started saying how I was keeping her dishonest by protecting her. Told me I was a queer boy to be protecting my mother so much."

Jed said nothing more, just looked across the town of Rockhill as if he was memorizing the patterns.

"Why don't you come stay with me for a while? Delores wouldn't mind."

"And then that leaves Mama and Sally. I can't do that to them. If I'm not there, he'll just be harder on them."

"What if I hang out at your place more?"

I used to spend more time with Jed. So many things had changed in the matter of a few years. I should've been bringing things between us to some kind of closure, not tying knots. But I started thinking of how Sally's face looked when she talked to me about Jed.

"Not after what my old man said. He'll think I'm even queerer to need protection. No," he said. "Leave things the way they are. They'll have to work themselves out."

Looking at Jed, he didn't seem as afraid as he had when we were younger, so afraid of Ol' Joe Ball, so afraid of fathers, afraid of anything really. Sally was as scared for him as I was becoming.

"We better get going," Jed said when the sun lowered in the sky. The noises in the distance sounded like the snapping jaws of gators.

DRIVING

The gears of the Nova ground so loudly that I immediately eased off the gas. If Tom wanted to kill me, he would've already done it. A shadow crept in the rearview mirror. I stared at it for a moment, trying to make out its shape.

"Manz, watch it, you're swerving!" Jed yelled. A chill trailed down my back. The babbling voices turned to whispers, and then back into shouts.

When we approached Jed's street, I slowed down, dreading the thought of taking Jed back to his prison. "Listen, I have to pick Delores up, but I'll come back later if you need anything." I looked for Sally, but I didn't see her through the blinds.

When Jed slammed the door shut, the echo was amplified in my ears. I squeezed my eyes shut against the momentary pain. Everything was still too loud when I opened them. I stayed in the driveway a moment longer to see if I could catch a glimpse of Sally. She wasn't there.

I looked down at my watch: I was late picking Delores up, but when I got to the Mart, she wasn't waiting anywhere outside or near the front of the store.

She might be dead, I thought. Jay Jackson might've done it, but I was the one who'd left her alone with him. I started feeling so ill, a putrid odor burned in my nose and I could taste it in the back of my nasal passage. It grew more intense with every second it took me to get inside.

When I opened the doors of the Mart, a bell rang and didn't seem like it would ever stop ringing. *Quiet!* Joanne, from the cash register, looked up at me.

I heard Delores's voice before I found her by the fryer. "Well I'll be," she said in response to a man as he lifted up his shirt to show her some sort of scar. She didn't even turn around to see it. Delores was alive.

The bell rang again when someone else entered and the bell kept on ringing and ringing.

"You can touch it," the guy told Delores.

Delores slid him a plate of food, but ignored the guy's offer. She still hadn't noticed me. The greasy spoon odor mixed with the ringing and made me feel like I was about to pass out.

"Mr. Jay," Joanne said, "Mr. Jay, you better get over here—the cash register is stuck again!" Joanne jerked the register drawer so hard she almost threw it to the ground.

Jay Jackson walked out of his office with a screwdriver in his hand. He didn't notice me in the store. I might've become invisible.

When I looked down the hall, light sprayed from Jackson's room. A voice commanded, *Go now*. It wasn't like Jed's dare. It was a command from the Messenger.

I had to listen.

I slid down the hall, the nerve endings in my fingers burning. I pushed my hand against the door, and holding my breath, I made my way into the room. *Hurry*, the voice said. Inside his office, there was a small TV playing the Mart's surveillance scenes. Rows and rows of VHS tapes were stacked on the side. They must've contained the town's history.

White files filled the shelves. Squinting, the black script on them spelled out names. They blended together in a dizzying pattern. Through the swirling pattern, two letters formed. OW.

"What are you doing back here?" Jay Jackson asked. My eardrums felt as if they'd exploded.

"Get out of here!"

Get out! The Man is coming. You will die! The voice of the Messenger sounded above all the other noise. Tears welled in my eyes. The burning sensation spread throughout my body and every nerve ending lit on fire. I felt as if I were burning alive. I dropped down to my knees. I had to block out the noise; I had to let go of the pain. I felt the shadows approach me.

"MANZ!" DELORES SAID, STANDING above me. Her red hair dangled in loose curls. I opened my eyes and the noise grew louder, but the burning sensation faded.

Even though I was coming to, Delores struck me across the cheek. "Pull it together, baby. Wake up!"

"What happened?" I asked, afraid I might die like the Messenger said I would.

"You were in this back hall when Mr. Jackson saw you standing near his door. He said something to you and you passed out. What happened? What were you doing?" She was talking so loud and fast my head reeled, trying to follow her questions.

"Be quiet," I said in a low voice. She brought her hand up again, as if to smack the shame right out of me. But she placed it on my forehead and leaned over to kiss me.

When I saw Jay Jackson, his eyes were bulging from his face, growing larger and larger as if in anticipation of Delores inflicting pain on me. He was a murderer. A serial killer. His eyes were about to bulge out of his skull. The fetid odor still lingered in the room. The names on all the files were his victims.

"It's too noisy in here," I said to Delores. How could she stand the noise and the smell?

"Everyone get back to work!" Jay Jackson yelled. Even customers listened to his order and went about picking out gum and lotto scratchers.

"What's happening to you, Manz?"

I couldn't answer Delores, but I stared at her, worried her eyes might bulge like Jay Jackson's did. I'd never seen anything like it before.

"I haven't felt so scared since . . . " Delores couldn't finish her sentence.

There were so many ways to finish it. I turned away from her and felt the liquid in my eyes moving outward. The more I wanted to prevent it, the less my body fought the tears. Delores rubbed her hand on my back when I turned away from her.

Stop this! I yelled inside. *Stop this!* But I couldn't.

I turned to Delores. "I don't hate you." But my eyes didn't meet hers. Knots and kinks formed in the rope I'd tried to sever. At that moment, it felt like a noose around my neck.

"You need help," Delores said as she helped me up. I should've given her a hug, but I kept my arms down by my side. Nothing used to be so hard.

"I was in the hot sun hiking with Jed all day. I haven't had anything to eat. Nothing is wrong." *Please don't make me confess anything else*, I thought. "I want to go home." And I really did.

"Where are the keys?" Delores asked. I dug them from my pocket and handed them over to her. "I'll be right back; don't go anywhere."

I sat in the hallway with my back pressed up tightly against the wall. Everything felt so intense around me. The bright candy bar wrappers and the fluorescent signs dangling from the ceiling—it was all enough to make my eyes burn like my body had earlier.

Another person walked into the Mart and the bell rang. The woman grabbed a bottle of water from a drink case.

I watched the cold air of the refrigerator case seep out, cooling the place down.

Delores grabbed her time card and clocked out. "Mr. Jackson said I could have the rest of the shift off to take care of you. Let's get home."

I squinted my eyes as I walked into the main area of the store. Joanne's eyes met mine for only a second before she looked down. Jay Jackson was nowhere in sight, but I knew he was watching me from the camera, just like he watched the whole town.

Delores unlocked the passenger side of the door and opened it for me with shaky hands. "Get in."

Numb, I followed her orders. She walked around the Nova and unlocked the driver's side. She adjusted the rearview mirror and slid the seat forward.

"I'll drive. I just need a moment." My mind kept replaying what I witnessed.

"I can do this," she said. "I can." Her hands shook on the wheel. The noise of her fear didn't help me sort anything out. I waited for the Messenger to say something, but he didn't. Maybe he knew I needed silence to take in what I'd seen in Jay Jackson's room. The names on the files formed the letters. I saw the letters form before my eyes. OW. Operation Wetback.

THE VOICES

The Man is coming, the voice of the Messenger boomed. This is what everything had been about—Delores and Tom might've been trying to protect me. I was part Mexican. They weren't. Maybe they were trying to protect themselves and wanted me gone. Too many maybes floated through my mind. One thing was for certain, though—Jay Jackson was behind the immigration stings and whatever was happening to me.

The voice of the Messenger kept repeating, *Listen. The Man is coming.* I tried to listen, but the voice of the Messenger combined with all the scattered noises was too much to take. I glanced at my watch. It was an hour and a quarter past midnight.

When I found the keys to the car, I started thinking I should drive across the Great Divide and let the people know that the authorities would be coming soon. The authorities would come, just like the Messenger said. I'm sure they knew—but I wondered if they were ready.

There was no longer a light creeping from underneath Delores's door. I put the keys back on the counter, deciding not to drive the Nova so I wouldn't wake her. She'd probably have been angry with me, especially after she put on a brave face for me and drove.

I slipped on my socks, the only pair left without holes in the heels or the toes. I pushed my feet down into my boots and laced them up. I knew it was going to be a long walk, but I had to let people know.

When I moved, the Messenger quieted, but my head began to pound. I felt as if I was wired to the railroad tracks and could sense the vibrations of a coming train. The night air bore a musty odor, which grew stronger as I approached the orchards. Everything felt like it was just waiting to happen.

A streak of a calico cat ran past me and I jumped back. When my eyes followed the cat, I noticed a shadow of a body running close to a fence.

"Who's there?" My voice sounded as if I was yelling into a canyon.

No answer.

"Tell me who you are! Stay away from me!"

No answer.

I ran, just like I'd wanted to bolt earlier. For a moment I worried I was running away from the ghost of my father, but I told myself it was the Border Patrol. The authorities were hunting me and I couldn't complete my mission to let people know they were coming. Jay Jackson had probably tipped them off and I needed to take cover. The burning sensations started all over again.

Out of breath, I reached Jed's house. I ran so far I might've lost the authorities, but I worried they could track where I went. There were no lights on in the house and I couldn't knock on the front door without waking Jed Sr. But I couldn't stand out there waiting to get caught either. I had to get inside and my only hope was Sally—her window faced the street.

At first, I extended my knuckles and tapped on the window. Nothing happened, so I tapped again. Finally, when I was brave enough, I made a fist and pounded on the window-pane. I ducked down in the shrubbery in case her father was the one who approached the window instead. My heart raced and I gulped breaths of air. A sheet of sweat clung to my body.

I knocked again, and this time Sally switched on a lamp and the shape of her thin body appeared in the window. I didn't duck down, but I couldn't control the fear that Mr. Parker was close behind, or worse.

"Manz," Sally said as she pulled the window open, "what in the world are you doing out here?"

"I'm not safe." Now that she was closer, Sally was more than just a shadow. "Please, can you let me in? I have to talk to Jed."

"He's asleep. We all are. Or at least I was." She stood

there for a moment as if wondering what she should do. "You don't look right."

"I need help. Please." She pried the window screen off.

"Get the corner," she said.

I lifted it up and crawled through the opening. I was about to bypass her room and head straight to Jed's, but Sally grabbed my arm.

"You have to tell me what's going on. You can't just come in here like this." Her hair stuck up on the side.

How could I tell her what was going on without risking her life? I started coughing to ease the itching sensation in my throat.

"Shhh." She patted me on the back like Delores had; the way she had after Gabriel died. "It's not your fault the baby died," she'd said to me.

WITHOUT ANY CONTROL, MY choking turned to tears. Sally wrapped her arms around me. My head sank into her shoulder so I wouldn't make any noise. She smelled sweet like nectar. Not anything like armpits or onions.

She thinks you're here to take advantage of her! a voice yelled. It wasn't the voice of the Messenger, but the voice sounded similar to mine. *She's going to smother you!*

I couldn't let Sally hear the voices, but it was probably too late. I'd infected her with my curse. I should've left, but I didn't want Sally to stop holding me. I couldn't let her, because if she did, I knew I'd fall to pieces.

"I hate myself," I said in a voice so low I felt my vocal

chords scrape against each other. "I hate myself so much." She didn't loosen her grip.

She thinks you're worthless! Worthless, worthless, worthless! the voice chanted.

"People have been telling me I'm going to die."

Sally pulled away from me and grabbed my arms. She stared into my face. "What?" she asked. Her forehead scrunched up. "Who would do that?"

"I can't tell you who," I said. "I've already put you and your family in enough danger. But they've been telling me I'm going to die. I think the authorities are tracking me."

"The authorities know what's going on?" Sally adjusted her oversized gray T-shirt. I'd left a wet spot on her shirt from my tears and sweat.

"I'm not certain, but I've got my suspicions. I couldn't be alone. I'm worried about Jed too."

"Why would someone want to hurt you?"

The volume of the buzzing and mumbling increased. I'd said too much. *She doesn't believe you!*

"I don't care!"

She thinks you're worthless. Worthless! WORTHLESS!

"You're going to wake everyone up," I said to the voice.

"Are you okay?" Sally grabbed my hand tightly. "Manz, what's going on? You're talking to yourself."

"You couldn't hear him?"

She's laughing at you! Ha ha ha!

"You don't hear the voices?"

"Just what we've been talking about, and then I heard

you say something to yourself. Are you having an asthma attack or something?"

She might be drugged, I thought. She couldn't hear the voices because she'd been drugged.

"Maybe," I said, going along with her theory. "I'm stressed and I'm freaking scared. I don't feel good."

"You have to get some help."

"I will," I said, lying. "I need to calm down. I started worrying about Jed and then," I said, pausing to sound more collected, "I overheard some . . . people . . . say I was in danger too. There's no reason to tell Jed about this. He needs his rest and it'll only stress him out. This is probably nothing. Please don't tell anyone about tonight."

Her eyes searched mine, wanting to trust me, I knew, but the glimmer of doubt was there.

Ha ha ha!

"I . . . I . . . just got scared. I needed someone to talk to and this was the first place I thought of."

Sally laughed. "It wouldn't be my first choice."

"You promise?"

She hesitated for a moment and then promised me. I told her I should get going. She looked outside and realized I didn't have the car.

"Stay here for a little while, to catch your breath at least." Sally left the room and came back with a glass of water, and I felt torn about whether I should drink from it. *She could be the enemy*, I thought, but I didn't want to leave. I set the glass of water by the window ledge and ignored the pools of sweat collecting all over my skin. Sally nudged her body near mine and leaned her weight into me. If I were to move, she would've fallen. She grabbed my hand and squeezed it.

We sat together like this until my body ached because I was too afraid to move; the noise might've returned and the moment would've been lost.

"I should get going," I said when my muscles froze. She'd fallen asleep. Maybe it was from the drugs.

"Are you sure?" Sally yawned.

"I feel safer." And in a way I did. "Remember our promise," I said when I popped the screen of the window back on.

"Don't worry." After Sally closed the window, she gave me an encouraging smile.

She lies!

The voices calmed as I moved again. I checked everywhere. Nobody was following me.

BECAUSE . . .

The sound of an engine churning made me jump awake. The smell of coffee filled the house. I rushed to the window. But Tom's truck wasn't outside and I realized the noise was only the train passing through Rockhill.

A long yawn brought tears to my eyes, and when I rubbed them, I dug at the crust formed in the corners. How long had I been asleep? I thought back to earlier that morning and it felt like a dream, but I distinctly remembered the weight of Sally's head on my shoulder.

I yawned again and entered the bathroom to run a hot shower. I had over an hour before I had to pick up Jed and I ached for a shower. I wondered if Sally would be true to her promise. The water almost stung as it hit my skin.

You know why they hate you?

"What?" Standing in the shower, I had an awful sensation

that someone was watching me. I flung the shower curtain open. No one was there.

They hate you because . . .

"Why?"

You know why they hate you?

They hate you because . . . the voice said again and again.

"Tell me!"

You know why they hate you?

They hate you because . . . ha ha ha!

"Shut up!"

With soap still on my skin, I flew out of the shower. I slipped on the bathmat and slammed to the ground. A pain in my arm shot down to my wrist. The voice laughed as I struggled to get up.

"Are you okay in there?" Delores asked.

"I'm fine," I said above the racket of the voices.

Ha!

I couldn't keep carrying on like this. I had to get out of here. Why hadn't I left when I had the chance?

You're too scared. Scared!

I tossed my clothes on and rushed out of the bathroom. I didn't brush my teeth and didn't comb my hair; I just got out. A cloud of steam followed me.

Delores stood outside the door. Her face seemed especially pale with the plume of steam surrounding her. "Who were you talking to in there?"

I could tell she heard the voices when I looked at her. She was testing me.

"Nobody. Just singing." Why couldn't she admit she heard the voices too?

"I have to ask you something, Manz," Delores started to say, but I pushed past her to enter my room. "Were you trying to hurt yourself?"

"No!" I was too transparent. I had to listen to the voices, but I couldn't talk back to them. No, I couldn't. Not with so many people watching me, judging me. I slammed the door shut and blared my stereo until it was time to pick up Jed. We had the fence to finish. It seemed like forever since we'd worked on the fence. Time didn't seem real anymore. Nothing did.

Delores tied on her apron when I come out of my room. Her dyed red hair was twisted up in a clip and the ends were fanned out.

"You look nice," I said, hoping she'd forgotten our argument earlier.

"I called Dr. Riason."

"Why?" The voices cackled.

"I can't lose you like I lost your father." She sipped on her coffee. When she tipped the cup, the smells floated in my direction. The whiskey smelled stronger than the coffee.

"There are other things you should be worrying about. Make yourself an appointment. You couldn't go nine months without drinking. Not even four!"

"Don't you dare turn this on me! Even if I would've stopped drinking completely, it wouldn't have made a difference. Don't you understand that? I want what's best for you. The appointment is for Thursday."

"I'm not going." Delores was lying to me—she was going to hand me over to the authorities. I knew that's what she intended to do.

"I'll go with you. Please."

I scratched at the vinyl tablecloth to keep from looking in those eyes of hers. Maybe she was getting drugged too, like Sally, but I didn't tell her.

Delores buried her face in the coffee mug. I scratched an itch above my eye and tiny flakes of skin fell from my face as if in slow motion.

Because . . . because . . . because, the voice said. I tried to ignore it, but I couldn't. She hated me because . . . there were too many possible answers.

"I have to pick up Jed. I'll drop you off," I said, injecting as much enthusiasm as I could into my voice.

"I still don't think it's safe." She dangled the keys from her finger and made a tight fist around them, locking up my freedom. "I'm sure Joanne wouldn't mind picking me up for work. She's already dropping me off tonight after we go out."

"What about Jed?" I told her about my job at Darby Guest Ranch. I needed the money. There wasn't enough time to wait for Jed to walk over here and then for us to cross the tracks. "Please Delores, please don't take this away from me."

"Then go to the appointment."

Delores stared at me, her eyes growing large like Jay Jackson's. I turned away. She was winning—defeating me.

"I'll go! Just let me drive." Inside, a voice laughed. I'd be long gone by Thursday.

"Are you sure you feel safe enough to drive?"

"I'm fine. If this is about the other night at the Mart, I already told you, I didn't have anything to eat. I'd hiked all day and wasn't feeling good." I looked her in the eyes, my final convincing piece of evidence. Her eyes were back to normal. "Besides, I've always listened to you. I don't drive far." I twitched. Maybe the reason Delores let me drive with only a permit was to give the Operation Wetback authorities a reason to take me to jail. Then they'd dispose of me.

FREAKING OUT

Sirens sounded so loudly all of Rockhill must've heard, but there were no flashing lights from speeding emergency vehicles. The OW authorities were coming for me. Delores had done the unthinkable—she'd turned me in. I craned my neck to look through the windows.

The Man is coming, the Messenger said.

"I know," I answered without holding back. I felt relief to hear his voice alone without the others. The sirens faded. Border Patrol and the police must've gotten distracted. For now.

I got back to my task: driving to Jed's. For a moment, I wasn't even aware I was driving. I couldn't afford to be so careless. Delores probably had the Nova wired—that's what Tom must've done to it.

When I got to Jed's, I honked the horn and rolled down the window. I couldn't bring myself to look at Sally's window. Not after our conversation. I didn't even look in the direction of the door, in case she came to check on me.

A hot wind blew through, scurrying up loose dirt. The branches of the trees rubbed up against each other, rustling the leaves together. *They hate you*, the blowing leaves whispered.

My hand slammed on the horn again, and this time I looked at the door to see where Jed was. I would've been satisfied to see Sally.

Hate you . . . Hate you . . . the leaves said when another small gust blew through. I stared at the orchard, and watched Jed Sr. walking through the trees. The trees stood stiff around him, and in the spaces between the crowded leaves, triangles formed out of the darkness.

I turned my eyes away and looked back toward Jed's house. Sally wasn't looking through the blinds. Why wasn't anyone there to witness it? Finally, Jed came out of the house.

"What took you so long?"

"You're early," Jed said. "I was helping Dad in the orchard. But he said I wouldn't have to work in the orchard much longer. He didn't even complain when I told him we were going out."

"What about Sally?" I asked, though I shouldn't have. I covered my eyes with my palms for even bringing her name up. When I started the engine and pressed the gas pedal I cringed, half expecting the sirens to return.

"Dad doesn't really give a lick what she does, that's the funny part. He just buys her more books and then complains when she's not cooking in the kitchen or scrubbing dishes like Mama."

"Did she say anything to you?"

"About what?"

I shrugged. Concentrate on driving, I told myself. Concentrate. "Did you notice anything in the orchard?" I asked Jed, disobeying my order to concentrate.

"No, it just looks like rain. What is this? Twenty questions?"

Hysterical laughter pealed from my mouth.

"You think that's funny?"

This question only made me laugh more. I wasn't paying attention to driving and I swerved in the road.

"Is Delores doing more than drinking these days?"

"Why?" I asked, the laughter washing away. *Focus!* Did he know something I didn't?

"It's like you're high."

"I haven't slept much. Tom will be gone for a while," I said, trying to get him to change the subject.

"What's new?" Jed responded in an irritated voice. I didn't bother explaining to him that I was the one who drove Tom off. Maybe he wouldn't be coming back. Somehow, I managed to drive us to the corner.

My eyes kept glancing around for any authorities while we waited for Smithson Darby. The wind blew grit in our faces and whipped around us.

Finally, the Silverado arrived. Smithson Darby rolled his window down and his eyes, his triangular eyes, looked at me with disgust. "Rain's coming, you boys just wait and see. You finish digging up the rest of them posts and finish the fence." He licked his finger and stuck it out of the truck to chase the wind. "It's going to be one hell of a storm."

In the truck bed, I held onto the lining and waited for the voices to speak, but they said nothing. Instead, my ears filled with the whistling sirens of the wind. Even when we reached the ranch, the wind whistled in my ears.

"When was the last time we were here?" I asked Jed when we got to work. We didn't have much left to rebuild.

"Just last week. Why?"

"Seems like it's been forever." I wondered why it felt like months and not days. A low boom of thunder sounded miles off in the distance. "You hear that?"

"Bet Rockhill won't see one drop of rain. It's like it's about to rain, but the clouds get constipated."

A storm is coming, the Messenger repeated, but it wasn't just his voice, it was a chorus of all the others.

"Yep, it is. A storm's coming."

WALKING TO LUNCH, I got shaky thinking about Vanessa. When we entered the dining hall, Vanessa was too busy smiling and passing glasses to notice us at first. I tried convincing myself I wasn't hungry, but the grumbling from my stomach was too much to ignore.

When we slid our trays down in her direction, her smile wilted. She handed us each a glass of water. No sweet tea.

"Why haven't you called me?" she asked. She crossed her arms over her chest. Her elbows made triangles out of her strong arms.

"So what's your excuse?" Jed asked, imitating Vanessa's

posture. He tapped his foot in feigned aggravation.

I ignored Jed and whispered to her, "OW. It's back in force. Make sure you tell everyone you know. You have to."

She crunched up her face, and asked, "What?"

"You heard me. I want you to be careful. Tell your father. I have some business I need to take care of," I said, ending our conversation. I grabbed a sealed bag of potato chips and sat down. Since they were sealed, I didn't think they'd be poisoned.

Jed rushed over to me. "What in the world was all that about?"

"Trying to warn her."

"You're freaking me out, Manz. You really are." Jed's teeth looked much too large for his mouth and his eyes looked much too large for their sockets.

"You're the one freaking me out, Jed." I shoved the chips into my mouth so fast that they scraped the back of my throat going down. "Hurry up." I threw the bag out and practically ran back to work. I wanted to get away from them all.

Jed ran after me. "Wait!"

WHEN I GOT OUTSIDE, the massive thunderheads had dulled the sun's brightness.

As I dug out one of the last rotting posts, my shovel struck cement. I started digging to the left of the post, and even angling the shovel in, but the post didn't budge. When I dug at the hole again, I saw something whitish gray exposed in the mud, something that looked like the top of a skull. I dropped down to my knees to look.

"Jed!" I yelled. "Jed!" I felt myself continuing to scream, though I wasn't sure if any sound was coming out.

Jed rushed over. "You okay?"

I pointed down at the earth. "A skull! You see it?"

Jed squatted down, almost as if in prayer. "You're right."

"You see it too?" I asked again.

"Good God, I see it too. Stop flipping out!"

AUTHORITIES

A roll of thunder rumbled again in the distance. The storm moved closer.

What have you done? a voice asked. *What have you done?*

"I haven't done anything!" Thankfully, Jed didn't respond. He crouched down.

"It looks real," he said. Looking at it, I had no doubt in my mind.

Real, the voice repeated. *What have you done?* The muttering around me filled my ears like the roar of a tornado.

"Maybe this is some ancient burial ground," Jed said.

I paced four steps up, four steps back. *A Mexican burial ground*, a combination of voices said. It was Loco's voice, the voice of the Messenger, and the voice without a name speaking all at once.

Jed grabbed a handful of dirt before standing up and let it slip through his fingers after examining it. The dirt flew diagonally in the wind. "You think there are other body parts around here?"

"I don't know." I kept pacing—four steps up, four steps back.

"Robert Oshay killed those kids a while back, remember hearing about his arrest? They never found the head and the hands of the girl. We have to tell someone."

"Like the authorities? Do we have to?"

"This could be huge." Jed's eyes bulged. They inflated in his sockets, ready to burst.

The mumbling and my thoughts churned wildly. What if there were other body parts out here? What if Smithson Darby planned for us to find the skull? What if he worked with Jay Jackson to set me up? Maybe it was the skull from a Mexican who was murdered.

Murdered. The part of Operation Wetback that no history book would talk about.

Bile collected at the back of my throat and I couldn't even stand up. My vomit splattered in the dirt.

What have you done?

"Are you all right?" Jed asked.

What have you done?

"Fine. Fine. Jed, don't rub your eyes," I said.

Raindrops started to fall, howling as they hit the ground. Jed walked away from me, away from the burial ground. The raindrops fell like bullets exploding from a soldier's gun. I started to run after Jed.

"Where are you going?" I yelled.

"We've got to tell someone."

I knocked on the door of the Big House even though I was so afraid. I had to show Jed I was in control. When I knocked again, the *Welcome* sign dropped to the ground. Smithson Darby flung the door open as I bent over to pick it up.

"What is this? You boys trick or treating? You ain't afraid of the rain, are you?"

"I hope it's a trick in the ground out there," Jed started to say, but then paused. "We found a skull. It might be human."

Smithson Darby scratched his nose. He chuckled. "You boys think you're funny?"

"We got to go quickly or the rain will fill the hole," Jed said.

"If this is some sort of joke . . . " Smithson Darby said while he grabbed a raincoat, but he didn't finish his threat as he followed us.

Stay quiet, the voices warned. I shielded my eyes with my hands to protect them from the rain, which fell in sheets.

Jed led Smithson Darby to the spot near the fence. The hole I dug started to fill with blood-colored mud. I thought of which tubes of Delores's paint it might take to create the same color. Red. A touch of yellow and a dab of black.

Jed leaned down and scooped some of the mud out, revealing the skull. The mud and the drops of blood dripped down from his hands.

Stay quiet.

"Balls be hung. You boys might be right," Smithson said, squatting close to the spot where I'd vomited. "Looks just like a skull." His eyes seemed to search the ground of the

Darby Guest Ranch, wondering what else might lie beneath.

Secrets, the voices chanted, *SECRETS*.

"Boy, you all right?" a voice asked. There were too many voices to distinguish any of them.

"You going to get sick again?" Jed asked.

My stomach lurched as more fluids came up. "I have to lie down." My throat burned and the sky swirled with raindrops.

AN HOUR PASSED, THOUGH it felt longer. I sat on a stiff couch in the Big House, staring at my boots to avoid the black-and-white photos of old people, plus everyone that kept coming and going.

"So tell me what happened," a man who looked like Vanessa's dad said. I stared at the gun in his holster and his Crockett County Sheriff's uniform. Engraved on his nameplate was Deputy Jerrett. The rain tapped and spat wildly off the tin roof of the Big House.

Don't trust him. He looked like he could be Mexican. *He's a good guy*, I tried convincing myself.

"We've been working, well, helping fix the fence . . . "

SHUT UP! You can't trust him. I felt time swirl away in a wash of colors.

"You with me here?" the sheriff said. "You were saying . . . "

Pull it together! "I was out there digging and that's when we found the skull. Why are there bones out here?" *Concentrate!*

Don't say anything or you'll die.

I wanted to blurt out the truth. I wanted to tell him about

being watched and about the awful noises and voices I'd heard. I wanted to tell him about everything I knew regarding Operation Wetback. I thought of the letters on the sign and on the tray and the connection made me sick to my stomach again.

What have you done?

"I haven't done anything," I said to the voices.

"Is there any other information you have?"

"I don't know anything about the skull. My friend and I found it, that's all." But it wasn't all. I held back from telling him everything. Deputy Jerrett nodded his head, and his eyes blazed at me as he walked off.

Jed whispered something to the deputy sheriff—he was definitely trying to frame me. Even the voices were trying to frame me. I couldn't trust anyone, not even the Messenger.

Other officials walked in and out of the Big House wearing bright yellow rain gear. Each time they passed through, they eyeballed me. Jed followed them around, listening to every word they said. When he glanced over at me, sitting on Smithson Darby's couch, I could tell he thought I was worthless scum.

I stared out of the old window, trying to hide from them and the voices. The rain slowed to a steady rhythm, but the thunder increased. The windowpanes rattled. The storms turned the sky black, but when I looked at the clock, it showed eight-fifteen P.M. I thought I was late before I remembered Delores was going out.

"Are you feeling better?" Jed asked.

"Yeah," I said even though I wasn't. My best friend had turned on me for good.

"You think it's real?" Jed's eyes finally shrank. I shrugged and hoped not.

"I've got to get home," Jed said. "Deputy Jerrett volunteered to drive us back since Darby is busy, or we'll have to call someone to pick us up. I'm all for getting a lift now. You?"

I worried the authorities had brought in the Mexican-looking sheriff to get me to believe in them. Deputy Jerrett would drop off Jed and then take me away. I'd never be coming back.

"I'm walking home."

Jed laughed. "You'll be walking for days in this rain."

Be calm, just be calm, I thought. "Then drop me off first. I have to pick up Delores," I lied. "Promise me I'll get dropped off first."

Thankfully, Jed agreed.

Jed and I rode in the backseat of the patrol vehicle like criminals. The bars on the windows framed the world we passed. I bit the inside of my lips to keep myself alert and I rested my hand on the door. Jed and the deputy said nothing.

Don't trust them, the voices chanted in loops. The skin inside my lips popped open and blood mixed into my spit.

Jed kept his promise. Deputy Jerrett pulled over to drop me off by the Nova. "Want me to take you home from here?" I asked Jed. I worried I might be locked in the car when I flipped the handle up, but it opened up without a fight. The artillery of the rain fired so loud I couldn't hear what Jed said to the deputy.

Secrets!

"Are you coming or not?"

"No," he said. "I've got a ride."

Secrets!

"Fine." When I dashed to the Nova and got into the car it hit me. I was still alive.

PADRE NUESTRO

Before one roll of thunder stopped booming, the next streak of lightning filled the sky and a crack of thunder followed so loud it seemed to split atoms in the air.

You know why they want you to die?

"I know!" I yelled at the voices.

They want you to die because . . . the voices screamed, and then howled with laughter, timed perfectly with the explosion of thunder outside.

You know why they want you to die?

"Yes," I said, but they wouldn't listen. They repeated it over and over again, stopping each time at the word *because.*

I plugged my fingers in my ears and screamed, "God's bowling! God's bowling!"

The voices laughed at my attempts to mute them. *Ha! Ha! Ha!*

Lightning formed shadows inside the house each time

it struck. Even the splattered rain on the windows created triangular shadows on the walls. I closed my eyes, but kept seeing the skull buried in the ground.

From the window, a bolt of lightning reached across the sky, and branched out to the ground. The lights inside flickered. Tears welled up in my eyes from the fear of complete darkness. I couldn't be alone.

I picked up the phone and dialed the phone number Delores kept on the side of the fridge for emergencies. The line to the Mart beeped a busy beep. "God's bowling!" I said again, trying to overpower the voices.

I dialed once more and this time, Jay Jackson answered, "Hello?"

"Delores there?" I asked, trying to keep my voice steady. I spoke loud enough to talk over the other voices.

"Left a few hours ago," Jay Jackson said. "You doing okay, boy?"

I hung up the phone on him.

Operation Wetback . . . the voices whispered. *The Man is coming for you.*

Jackson was taping and watching me from a camera in the TV. I saw my reflection in the television and it started humming. Why did I call and let him know I was here? I grabbed the closest object I could find—Delores's vase. It crashed loudly as it hit the television, shattering upon impact. There would be cameras watching me, so I grabbed my suitcase and threw clothes into it and picked up an old pair of boots. There wasn't much else I needed. The voices shrieked in laughter, telling me I wasn't brave enough to leave.

The phone rang, and at first, it sounded like the voices were the ones making the noise, mocking my conversation with Jay Jackson. But the phone rang again and again and I knew it was Jay Jackson, angry I'd ruined his camera. Jay Jackson was calling, ready to send me to Mexico, ready to kill me.

Answer it, the voices yelled, but it was clearly the voice of the demanding Messenger. *Answer it!*

I picked up the phone, which felt cold in my hand. "Hello?" I waited to hear Jackson.

"Manz, come quick!" My stomach dropped to my toes and my toes weren't grounded. I felt as if my hand held a fork and I'd stuck it deep into a socket.

"What happened, Sally?"

She'd been crying; I heard it in her voice. "Just come, Manz, come as fast as you can. The ambulance is on the way." Sally hung up.

Don't believe her. She's lying.

"She wouldn't lie!"

She's setting you up.

I knew I had to go. Despite the warning from the voices, I walked outside. The rain still pelted down and the rolling thunder continued. Water flooded down Allen Street in currents; it was several feet deep in some places. I opened the car door and tossed the suitcase in the backseat.

The Nova wouldn't start when I twisted the key. "Damn it!"

The voices snickered at my failed attempt. But I gave it

another try, holding it down and letting the wet engine rev up. Finally, it turned over.

It's a trap. Everyone thinks you're worthless. Worthless!

"Quiet!" My bellowing accomplished nothing. The voices continued to yell.

My foot stomped on the gas pedal and I gave it a hard kick. Water shot up into the wheel wells and stalled the Nova before it lunged forward. Sirens screamed from every street in Rockhill, but just like before, I didn't see flashing lights.

They're coming for you.

I was almost ready for them to come get me and let it be over. I turned the corner so sharp the back end of the car fishtailed.

A low water crossing forced me to slow down and the engine groaned. *Let me get there and let Sally be alive*, I thought. I finally saw the flashing lights.

An ambulance was parked outside Jed's house, as well as a patrol car. Red and blue lights whirled around in circles. I parked on the street in the flooding water. Looking away from the hideously bright lights, I noticed the apples on the trees. They were like beating hearts pulsating with ancient energy.

My feet trudged through the water as soon as I stepped out of the car. "Sally! Jed!" I cried out. The front door was cracked open and I darted in.

Run away from here, the voices commanded. *You're going to die. Die! DIE!*

I placed my fingers in my ears to block out the awful hollering. Sally saw me and ran over, blood dripping down her shirt. When I looked around the room, blood dripped from the authorities. Blood seeped from the ceiling and spilled out of the walls.

Then I saw Jed Sr. in a stretcher. An oxygen mask covered his face and emergency workers pounded his chest.

I finally spied Jed Jr. in handcuffs with his head down. It looked like a sheriff was reading him something. The rifle rested near his feet and Jed was covered in blood.

"You can't be here . . . " a deputy said. His uniform wasn't tan like the other uniforms—it was green and I realized he was Border Patrol. I watched his lips move, but I couldn't hear his words because of the crunching and the mumbling and the yelling.

Sally grabbed my arm and pulled me aside, "Jed shot him." She was no longer blue—now she was red. A deep bloody red. "Mama's hurt." Sally dripped in red. I felt like I would be sick all over again.

Don't believe her.

"She was trying to protect Jed because Dad was really laying into him. He told Mama to be quiet, but she screamed back. They were fighting because Dad sold the place—the orchard and everything. That was the secret. He kept hitting her. Jed got the gun."

Sally was a ghost, a bloody ghost. She didn't want to deceive me, I could tell.

She's lying. This is a setup, the combination of voices said. *A setup. None of this is real.*

Standing in front of her, a feeling came over me like I

was getting a glimpse behind the scenes of a movie. None of it was real. The folks from the ambulance kept wiring up Jed Sr. and wheeled him into the ambulance. I couldn't find Jed's mom. She was hiding, I knew it. More authorities and deputies entered the house and worked on setting the scene. But they stopped what they were doing and eyeballed me with disgust, then started nodding their heads and signing messages with their hands to each other. The sheriff kept reading to Jed, but when I looked at him, we made eye contact and I saw him smile. He'd set this up with Deputy Jerrett. They'd finally won.

The deputy wearing a Border Patrol uniform grabbed me by the arm, saying, "This is a crime scene. You have to leave the premises." He pulled me out the front door and away from Sally before I had a chance to tell her I forgave her. They had forced her into tricking me.

I balled my hand up in a fist and swung at the officer. My fist pulsed after making impact and the flaming sensation spread down my arms and up my neck. The Messenger's voice rose above the others and screeched, *Run!*

I took off before the officer had a chance to fully recover. I ran to the Nova and fumbled the keys in the ignition.

"Son of a bitch, start!" I turned the engine long and hard until it churned and choked.

You're going to die. Die. DIE.

My foot pressed so hard on the gas it felt as if it would slip through the rusted floorboard. Water sprayed out of the back tires, and for a moment, the car didn't go anywhere.

But I let off the gas and got the car in gear. I drove to Highway 90, my thoughts racing to my father's death. The authorities had staged his death as an accident just like they'd stage mine. It was all becoming clear to me.

The rain fell harder and the lightning continued to streak across the sky. The noise of the water under the tires was as loud as a rocket. Sirens and colors in the rearview mirror whirled around. Blue and red. Sally's colors.

Die. DIE!

I watched as the dials on the dash increased. The Nova started overheating and the authorities were too close. They'd catch up to me soon.

Run!

Water from the flooding creek completely covered the road. Fantasma Creek became a formidable body of water leading to freedom. I had to cross it. I had to get to Mexico. I had to get to safety.

Run!

I plowed the Nova into the creek and immediately felt the strength of the car wash away. The sheriff's car stopped before entering the flooded creek. I pulled at the door and tried to get out of the car, but the force of the water was too fast to control. Finally, I managed to kick the door open and swim out, but the flood's current pulled me down.

DIE!

I struggled to keep my head above water. Finally, I struggled up and gasped for air. I tried reaching out to grab something, but there wasn't anything within my grasp. My head bobbed completely under the water again, but it didn't silence the laughing voices.

"Help!" I screamed before the water pushed me completely under again. But there wasn't anyone to help. Their mission had been accomplished. My eyes opened wide with terror. I couldn't see anything. Not even shadows.

I prayed in Spanish, a prayer I remembered my father saying with me before going to bed. *"Padre nuestro, que estás en el cielo . . . "*

The lights were so bright, like the light shining into a cathedral—blue and red flashes whirled above me.

EXECUTION

The world was filled with silence. The room pulsed a bright fluorescent yellow white. A layer of fog covered my eyes, and when I attempted to speak, my voice was anchored deep beneath the surface.

When I tried sitting up, white sheets suffocated me, holding me down. My strength was diminished. Trying to move, I noticed a tube jutting out of my vein, injecting drugs from a bag hanging on a pole.

I tried talking again, but what spewed out was garbled and scratchy. I pulled at the wires in my hand and when I yanked them out, fluids and blood gushed from my vein.

Die, the voices whispered. An image of the skull at the ranch filled my mind. I couldn't let myself think of it or the blood dripping from Sally.

"Manz, you'll be okay," a woman said. I turned and stared at her, not noticing her until she spoke.

"You have to help me, Delores," I tried to say, but my voice was hoarse and I'm not sure she understood me. "Help." She had to understand.

"You're going to be just fine." Her voice was too shaky to sound reassuring.

"What are you doing here?" I asked her, but it sounded like babble. I couldn't speak right from all the drugs they'd shot into me. They were preparing me for execution and Delores was a witness. I saw the fear in her eyes.

Escape, the Messenger said. It was clearly only his voice this time. Delores stared at me, her large brown eyes too easy to read. She knew I wanted to run away.

Ripping the sheets off me, I began to stand up, but my head pounded and my legs felt numb. I felt numb all over.

Get out of here, the voices said, combined all together again.

I leaned out of the bed, and looked around the room. I was in some sort of infirmary or quarantine. My legs were too weak to run, but I walked as fast as I could out of the room.

Delores grabbed me around the waist. "You have to stay here! Help!"

Border Patrol officers rushed over to me, grabbed me by the arms, and carried me back to the room. The officers were disguised in hospital scrubs.

A Border Patrol officer dressed in a white doctor's coat walked into the room. A needle flashed in her hand. She pressed the syringe down and liquid squirted out. I could almost hear her laughing.

"Don't kill me! She's going to kill me!" I yelled, and faced

Delores. Her eyes wouldn't meet mine. The other officers, large men, pinned me down and rolled me over to my side.

"I'm Dr. Jabowski and you're in Crockett County Hospital's psychiatric ward," the woman with the needle said. "You're hallucinating, Isaiah, and this is going to calm you down."

"Murderers! Liars!" I cried with my face mashed into the bed. I continued screaming as the officer inserted the needle into my backside. The liquid stung as it entered my body. Immediately after, I squeezed the injection site to purge the poison. I began screaming about Operation Wetback and the lies they were telling me, but then the drugs made it too hard to struggle and I relaxed in my own puddle of drool. The voices laughed at me, but it felt too difficult to go on, so I closed my eyes and surrendered to the heaviness settling in.

SICKNESS

"Are you hearing voices right now?" Dr. Jabowski asked, sitting next to me in the yellow white room. They'd drugged me with antipsychotics, forcing me to talk. I was being forced to take prescriptions I didn't need.

"What are the voices saying now?" the doctor asked. Her questions were endless, but I liked to hear her voice. It reminded me of the feeling I got when I was around Sally. I pretended it was Sally's voice, not the voice of a doctor.

"Nothing," I said.

"When did the voices start?" Dr. Jabowski continued scribbling notes into my file. I tried not to worry that it was more evidence to use against me. It was a white file, like those I saw in Jay Jackson's room.

"I'm not sure. I have no clue how long I've been in here and how long ago they started." It felt good to be able to talk about the voices, but I was too scared to confess everything.

"You've been in here two months."

"Two months, are you sure?" I ran my hand over my face and felt the roughness of my chin. When I had looked into the mirror the day before, I winced at first, waiting for some awful reflection. I saw myself, though, and noticed how hollow I looked. Sort of like Delores in a way. My hair had grown long and stubble filled in the space above and below my lips.

"I have no reason to lie to you," the doctor said. "You were heavily sedated when you were transferred to the ward. The medication can distort things, as can your illness."

"Then why do I have to take it?" There were several times I had tucked the pills into my cheek, but I never got away with it.

"Everyone here wants to help you. The medication is the first step."

I was scared to trust her, but I needed to so badly if I wanted to get out of here.

"When did you first start noticing any changes?" Dr. Jabowski continued on with her questions. I had to remind myself how it felt to talk to Sally. I closed my eyes to remember her body leaning next to mine.

"After Gabriel died, I guess."

I talked to her about how excited Delores and Tom felt when they found out about the pregnancy. I told her about the decision Delores made to terminate. "The baby felt like a gift to me too," I said. "And then I had to lose him. If I'd only stopped her from drinking . . . "

Dr. Jabowski didn't tell me that anencephaly was genetic. She didn't tell me that Gabriel would've died regardless of Delores's drinking. She didn't try to tell me that it wasn't my fault. She listened to me talk, just like Sally would have.

I wedged my fingernail into my skin and gouged at it until both my fingertip and the skin underneath turned a bright red. The pressure was still there after I placed my hands on my clean pants.

"Have you had any recent thoughts about hurting yourself?"

"Not really. No more questions today," I said. The air in the room thinned and talking required more oxygen than my lungs were getting.

"You're making progress," Dr. Jabowski said. "I'm proud of you."

"HAVE YOU THOUGHT ABOUT hurting yourself?" Dr. Jabowski asked the next day, starting where we left off.

"Not at this moment." For a second I forgot the question. "But right as you walked into the room, the voices told me not to trust you."

"Why is that?" Dr. Jabowski asked.

"They said I'd die if I talked to you." I waited for a look of horror or disbelief to appear on her face, but it didn't. Instead, Dr. Jabowski nodded her head and wrote something in the file. The Isaiah Luis "Manz" Martinez file.

Looking at her more closely, Dr. Jabowski didn't seem like she could be a murderer. She looked like Delores in some ways, but not as skinny or as young, even when she smiled. Dr. Jabowski took her coat off before our sessions so she looked less like Border Patrol. It made her look more normal, easier to talk to.

"How did you respond to the voices?" she asked.

I shrugged. "I'm not dead, am I?"

"When can I see Delores?" I asked Dr. Jabowski. I hadn't seen my mother since I first arrived. I wasn't even sure if Tom had returned to Rockhill. He'd find a joke about what happened. He'd probably put on one of those bumper stickers on his truck or the Nova that said, "Out of my mind. Be back in a few. . . ."

"Soon," she said. "You'll see her soon. She's working with a caseworker right now, learning how to help you through this. That's what we're trying to do too. Have you been keeping your journal?" she asked.

My journal sat on my desk, untouched. "No." Dr. Jabowski didn't look upset at my defiance.

"How do you feel taking the Haldol?" she continued asking me her endless questions.

"Like shit. I don't feel better, if that's what you're asking. I can't sleep at night and my guts feel sick on top of things. You're poisoning me in here."

The doctor scribbled more notes in my file.

"We are working toward the goal of your wellness. Are the voices getting better or worse?"

"The same I suppose." But they weren't yelling at me like they were before. The head buzz was still there, but I didn't tell Dr. Jabowski any of this because I didn't want to answer more questions or take more medicine.

"Give it time," she said.

That's what everyone around here said—nurses, guards, and even the patients in my group sessions.

"There are other medicines to try, but we'll give the Haldol some time first." Time was just another thing that bordered on reality.

When I got back to my room, I wrote my first line in the journal. "If I don't cooperate I don't get to leave. I haven't been in as long as the people in group, but I want to get out of here."

Run away.

I ignored what I heard. I knew if I ran away, the problems would get worse and I'd die for sure.

In the journal, I drew a picture of myself inside an airplane. It didn't look nearly as good as the pictures Delores had painted. In the drawing, I sat in the seat and looked over my shoulder. My hair was past my shoulders and I had a full beard. Out a dark window, I saw a puff of a cloud and a few stars shining off in the distance.

TALKING

"Why don't you talk about why you're here, Isaiah?" a new therapist named Marty asked during our group session. I wasn't as comfortable talking to someone I barely knew, but I thought about what I kept writing in my journal. I wrote questions about why it had all happened and questions about Operation Wetback. I needed to leave the hospital, and talking was the key.

There were three other people my age in the group and we answered Marty's questions about our experiences and our thoughts. I tried not to concern myself with their problems—I didn't want to start growing roots here.

I looked at the other faces in our group therapy—Dom, Brianna, and Frank. I was the youngest of them all, but we were the "teen group." There were only four of us combined. There used to be another person, but she was discharged before I was admitted.

The guy named Dom put his hands to his lips and inhaled an invisible cigarette. When he placed his hands back in his lap, he exhaled loudly. He did this at every session.

"Dr. Jabowski says I have paranoid schizophrenia," I said to the group. Nobody was surprised. We went over these things every day. I guess I was informing Marty about myself. I hoped he didn't ask anything about Operation Wetback. I'd done enough talking about the events that led me here.

"What does this mean to you?" Marty asked.

"Dr. Jabowski says I'm delusional and my mind has created a web of false realities. She insists the voices aren't real—that they're part of my sickness."

"But what does this mean to *you*?" Marty continued. I ached to hear a question that I could answer with either a "yes" or "no."

"It's hard to say. The voices are real to me."

"Who is to say what's real and what isn't?" Dom asked, putting his cigarette down. He held it between his fingers and set it on the edge of the table. He fanned the smoke that only he saw.

"When you think about the world," Brianna began, and then stopped for a moment to think. "No, not just the world, when you think about the planets," she said, "they look like atoms. No, molecules? Earth is the proton. Life is the neutron and the moon is the electron. Each planet is its own molecule.

"Space is just a bunch of these things put together. We

could be molecules underneath a giant's fingernail. That's how meaningless this all could be."

"Interesting thoughts," Marty said. The voices started to laugh. I could tell Marty wanted to use her name, but he didn't know it.

He didn't know us either, other than what we became in a chart to read about. We hardly knew each other and we certainly didn't know ourselves.

"Do you think the voices are real?" Marty continued. The answer to the question was a "yes" or a "no." I knew what answer he was looking for, but I didn't give it.

"They're like Dom's cigarettes," I said.

Dom reached over to the table and picked up his cigarette. I could almost smell the smoke.

"What if the voices are real and what everyone sees as reality is really the delusion?" Brianna asked. Her question went unanswered.

"I guess I'd like proof of what is real and what isn't," I said to everyone in the group.

"What if everyone else is mental and we're the ones who are sane?" Brianna asked. Out of all of us, she'd been there the longest. Dom exhaled his cigarette louder to try to distract her.

"What do you mean by that?" Marty asked.

Brianna rambled about false realities, thinking the question might've been directed at her. Frank, the quiet guy, tapped his feet on the floor.

Marty wrote down the things she said, though to me,

there wasn't much importance to her words. That's all they were—words. It was like, if they could get you to start talking more on the outside, the talking would quiet on the inside. I didn't want them to be right, but I started hearing my own thoughts again.

"What kind of proof are you looking for?" Marty asked. He slid his glasses up to the bridge of his nose.

These people tried in any way that they could to get us to talk. It was more talking than I'd done all my life, but I don't think talking could've prevented what happened to me and Delores and Tom. Or Loco.

Brianna continued on about scientific proofs that were created just to fool people. Marty kept listening.

While I was in the ward I realized my father had been sick—the same way that I was sick. Not exactly the same, but the triangles came together to make a square. A square is easier to measure than a triangle. I felt like I was starting to think like Brianna.

Delores could never fully accept Loco's sickness, or even Gabriel's. I guess I never believed my father was sick like this, just like I couldn't imagine a baby with no chance. How could there be diseases like that?

I thought back to those times my father sat still for so long. What about the times that he was there, but not available? What was he seeing? Who was he seeing? What was he hearing? What did shadows mean to him?

His nickname was something I never took seriously. Loco. Crazy. That left me, his legacy. What did Delores know that I didn't? I didn't want questions and talking. I wanted answers.

"Isaiah, are you hearing voices now?" the therapist asked. "Would you like to share with us what you're experiencing?"

"I'm thinking," I said. Frank tapped his right foot in a rhythm. Tap, tap tap, tap.

"I need some kind of evidence of what is real and what isn't. I need to know what happened and what didn't."

I waited for Brianna to start talking about perceptions and confusions, but she didn't. She looked at me instead, waiting for me to continue.

"I need to make squares out of the triangles." None of them asked what I meant, but I knew.

Silence filled the bright room, except for the scratching noise of the therapist writing in the chart. My chart. Frank tapped and tap-tapped and Dom finished his cigarette.

DREAMS

Delores walked into the ward and I barely recognized her. Her hair was cropped short and brown and framed her thin face.

"Do you like it?" she asked, running her fingers through her hair. I noticed paint streaks along her forearm. Those sad, hopeful eyes of hers looked at me, waiting for a response.

No, the voices answered and I kept myself from laughing. Dr. Jabowski said only I could hear them, but I wasn't sure how much of that I trusted.

"I do," I said and she looked pleased. "You've been painting again, haven't you?" I pointed at her arm.

"Yeah," Delores said. "It helps. Speaking of which, Mr. Jackson gave me extra hours and a bonus to help out. He even said when you get better that you've got a job if you want it."

"That's good." I swallowed hard.

"What are you painting?" I asked.

"Just making swirls like you did. Patterns, nothing really."

"You knew?"

Delores nodded her head. She was quiet for a moment before she started talking again. "Tom wanted to be here, but he had to take another job before we were allowed to visit." She handed me a stack of letters. About fifty of them.

The letter on the top read, "To Manzoil." I smiled.

"You look good, baby." Delores stood in the empty room, shifting her weight from one leg to another.

"You're a crappy liar."

She tried to laugh, but couldn't force it out. Delores was like me; most of the time she held her laughs in.

"Tom did want to be here. I'm not lying about that."

I nodded my head in acknowledgement. She sat on the edge of my bed, like old times. There we were, in the hospital room together, the silence transformed into humming.

"Are you sure you want these?" Delores asked, opening up her deep purse. She pulled a folder out and placed it into my hands. She rested her hand on top of mine. "Your doctors thought this might be helpful. I don't see how."

"I need it." I squeezed her hand, and then flipped the folder open. I ran my fingers over the black ink of the newspaper clippings. A smear transferred onto my hand, dripping like blood. The voices thought it was hilarious.

It's not blood, I told myself. I wiped the ink stain on my pants and focused my attention back to the clippings. I spread them out before me. Proof.

I'd read the articles in depth when Delores left, but I shuffled through the titles:

"Domestic Abuse Strikes Again at Parker Place"

"Father Survives Shooting"

"Teen Nearly Drowns in Flash Flood"

It was real. We'd gone over it in therapy, but the writing made it history. I started flipping through the papers, trying to escape the loud humming and the burning sensations ripping through my body.

Real. The voices snickered. *Real.*

"Mrs. Parker is doing all right. Too bad the old man is all right too," Delores said.

Die!

I twitched my head and stuck a finger in my ear. "How is Sally? What about Jed?"

"They're staying with an aunt in Selma. The charges against Jed were dropped, but his father is awaiting trial."

Delores reached out and dug in her purse. "Sally said you'd know what this means." She handed me a clump of dried mistletoe. I held it carefully in my palm, thinking of all the roots ripped right out of the orchard. "Vanessa wanted me to give you this too. She said she and her family want you to get better soon."

Vanessa had carved me a heart-shaped apple and painted it red. I folded my hands around it. "Thanks."

"You don't remember anything?" Delores asked. From the expression on her face, I knew she didn't believe me.

171

They're all lies, the voices tried convincing me, but I doubted it.

"There was blood everywhere when I got to Jed's. Blood even dripped from the walls. They were setting me up. They were all in it together setting it up. They wanted me to die."

"You're going to get better, you know," Delores said, more to herself than me.

Dr. Jabowski told me I may never get well. Time will tell. Loco never did—get better, that is. I thought of using him as an example, but I couldn't wipe the hope out of my mother's eyes.

Tell her, the Messenger commanded. *Tell her you're not sick.* But I tried to ignore him.

"Tom and I will be back soon. You'll be out of here in no time, you'll see," Delores said, hugging me close to her small frame. I couldn't ignore the scent of whiskey.

She grabbed her purse and straightened out her skirt.

"What about the skull?" I asked before she left. "The one Jed and I found working at the Darby Guest Ranch?"

"If I remember right, the news reporter said police are continuing to investigate."

Liar!

Despite what the voice said, I knew she wasn't lying. I didn't need proof, though I needed to talk to Jed, and to Sally too.

I'll be getting out soon, I told myself.

After Delores left, I didn't write in the journal. I didn't log my feelings or quote what the voices said. Instead, I read through Tom's letters, mostly jokes.

I drew a sketch of Vanessa's apple. I had to think of something special to give to her.

THE LIGHT IN THE nurses' station fed into my room. If the nurses knew I wasn't asleep, they'd give me more medicine. I was already floating.

When I closed my eyes, I could hear Tom's truck outside, the engine gurgling and the horn honking. The smell of oil hung in the thick night air. The scene blurred, but I watched myself, from a different perspective, drifting out of bed and into the truck.

Tom's voice laughed when I landed in the truck beside him. "Took you long enough."

I whooped loudly as Tom sped along the highway. The speed filled the pit of my stomach with excitement.

But as Tom turned around a bend, my body slipped from the seat and started floating out the window and back. Back. Back to the bed. I watched as my body filled the space under the white sheets.

"You're hallucinating," a nurse above me said.

I laughed hysterically, the euphoric sensations still tingling. "I'm dreaming."

The nurse forced medication on me. "Please, no," I said.

I closed my eyes and tried to get the feelings back. I'd never experienced anything like it before. I had to get back on the road with Tom. *I'm going to be his second seat driver*, I thought.

When the darkness returned at last, I was on my way out

of Rockill and Tom laughed so hard he had to hold his guts in place. I was on my way. Away from Rockhill. Away from the nothingness and the everythingness. Away from it all. But Tom said, wherever you go, you come back somewhere.

I knew there was still another border to cross.

ABOUT THE AUTHOR

Photo by Tim Kingsbury

Jessica Lee Anderson is the author of *Trudy*, which won
the Milkweed Prize for Children's Literature in 2005. While
her experiences have ranged from teaching to selling
computers to coordinating a vision therapy clinic, her
lifelong passion is writing literature for children. She lives
near Austin, Texas, with her supportive husband, Michael,
and two peculiar dogs, Buster and JoJo.

ALSO BY JESSICA LEE ANDERSON

Trudy
A novel of learning to adapt to change

"Jessica Anderson has a gift for capturing profound emotion in very accessible language. *Trudy* is a beautiful novel of loss and love that will appeal to a broad audience." —*Twin Cities Daily Planet*

"As Trudy deals with the issues of adolescence—fitting in, making new friends, and figuring out algebra—she must face something her classmates will not soon experience in the gradual decline of a loved parent." —*VOYA*

Lately, Trudy has begun to notice that strangers often mistake her parents, who are almost seventy, for her grandparents. As if that doesn't set her far enough apart, she is struggling to adapt to middle school and all its challenges—new classes, new teachers, and new friends. She is bombing math class, and Ashley, her former best friend, has ditched her for a new crowd. Trudy misses the way her life used to be in grade school, when she felt like she fit in.

After Trudy makes a new best friend at Benavidez Middle School—the straight-talking Roshanda—and has her first serious crush on a boy, it seems like life with lockers and class schedules might not be too bad. But when Trudy's father starts to act funny—forgetting Trudy's name and putting away groceries in the bathroom—she and her mom embark on a quest to find out what's wrong with Pop and if anything can be done.

Both heartwarming and honest, *Trudy* is the story of a family wrestling with the meaning of love while they come to grips with the pain and disorientation of Alzheimer's.

Available from your local bookseller or www.milkweed.org.

MILKWEED EDITIONS

Founded in 1979, Milkweed Editions is one of the largest independent, nonprofit literary publishers in the United States. Milkweed publishes with the intention of making a humane impact on society, in the belief that good writing can transform the human heart and spirit.

JOIN US

Milkweed depends on the generosity of foundations and individuals like you, in addition to the sales of its books. In an increasingly consolidated and bottom-line-driven publishing world, your support allows us to select and publish books on the basis of their literary quality and the depth of their message. Please visit our Web site (www.milkweed.org) or contact us at (800) 520-6455 to learn more about our donor program.

Milkweed Editions, a nonprofit publisher, gratefully acknowledges sustaining support from Anonymous; Emilie and Henry Buchwald; the Patrick and Aimee Butler Family Foundation; the Dougherty Family Foundation; the Ecolab Foundation; the General Mills Foundation; the Claire Giannini Fund; John and Joanne Gordon; William and Jeanne Grandy; the Jerome Foundation; Constance and Daniel Kunin; the Lerner Foundation; Sanders and Tasha Marvin; the McKnight Foundation; Mid-Continent Engineering; the Minnesota State Arts Board, through an appropriation by the Minnesota State Legislature, a grant from the Wells Fargo Foundation Minnesota, and a grant from the National Endowment for the Arts; Kelly Morrison and John Willoughby; the National Endowment for the Arts; the Navarre Corporation; Ann and Doug Ness; Ellen Sturgis; the Target Foundation; the James R. Thorpe Foundation; the Travelers Foundation; Moira and John Turner; Joanne and Phil Von Blon; Kathleen and Bill Wanner; and the W. M. Foundation.

MINNESOTA
STATE ARTS BOARD

NATIONAL
ENDOWMENT
FOR THE ARTS

A great nation
deserves great art.

TARGET.

THE McKNIGHT FOUNDATION

Interior design by Steve Foley

Typeset in Emona

by Steve Foley

Printed on acid-free Glatfelter paper

by Friesens Corporation